Slow Monkeys
and other stories

Slow Monkeys
and other stories

Jim Nichols

Carnegie Mellon University Press
Pittsburgh 2002

Book design: Katherine Bouwkamp
Cover design: James Mojonnier

Library of Congress Control Number 2002101290
ISBN 0-88748-379-8 Pbk.
Copyright © 2002 by Jim Nichols
All Rights Reserved
Printed and Bound in the United States of America

10 9 8 7 6 5 4 3 2 1

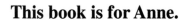

This book is for Anne.

"The Rain Barrel" originally appread in *Esquire*; "Jade" in *Paris Transcontinental*; "Orion" in *Jam Today*;"Mackerel" in *Karamu*; "Slow Monkeys" in *The Clackamas Review*; "C'est Le Vie"in *American Fiction, Vol. 9*; "Jon-Clod" in *River City*; and "Loons" in *Andy's Doghouse*.

Table of Contents

Magic

The last time I was in jail, the Sheriff suggested that if I were to jump off the Bucksport Bridge, it would save us both a lot of future trouble. And I tell you, it was starting to sound like a good idea. I even walked out the trestle a few times and looked down into the gorge. I dropped rocks over the side. It took about four seconds for the rocks to fall, and I remembered from physics class that it would be the same for me, despite the difference in mass.

Four seconds.

In school I'd been happy enough. Under my yearbook photo: Always Quick With A Smile Or A Trick. That's because I was the school magician. And I was still capable of putting on a show. I could make coins, handkerchiefs, cigarettes disappear.

I just couldn't get rid of my gloom.

I lived in a trailer park and, when I could rouse

myself, drove an airport taxi for cash. For days at a
stretch, though, I wouldn't leave the trailer, and when I
finally did it was only to walk to the bridge.

It was breezy over the river.

The bridge shimmied beneath my feet. When I
dropped the rocks they fell straight down until the river
breeze caught them and then swung outward and
plunged at an angle into the water. I would watch those
rocks and sometimes I would be only a thought or two
from swinging a leg up over that flaky green railing.

I had a friend named Bobby Kincaid. One night
after I'd missed work again he showed up at the trailer
with a bottle of Coffee Brandy and a gallon of milk.

"Enough of this," he said, barging past me inside.
"You're making me look bad."

"Come on in," I said. "Make yourself at home."

He stomped down to my little tin kitchen, dumped
half of the milk into my sink, emptied the bottle of
coffee brandy into what was left, put the cap on the
milk container and gave it a shake as he came back.

"I went out on a limb to get you that job."

"I know you did."

He sat down beside me and passed me the jug. A
Sombrero, the blueberry rakers called it. I took a gulp
and handed it back. We worked at it silently, and before
long the booze was half gone, and so were we.

"So what's the big deal?" Bobby said then.

"I wish I knew."

"All you gotta do is drive the damn car."

"It's not just work. I can't do anything."

"Was it jail?"

"Didn't help."

"What else?"

"Jeez," I said. "Pick a card." I waved a hand. A few feet to my left was the little kitchen nook, and to my right the bathroom. Clothes and magazines were stacked on every flat surface because I didn't have any closets. I couldn't fold the sofa out without moving a junky lampstand that stood against the opposite wall.

"You ain't the only one lives in a trailer."

"That doesn't help."

Somebody hollered from outside. It was the green trailer that sat kitty-corner to mine. They'd been party-ing for a couple of days, off and on.

Bobby laughed. "Somebody don't mind living here."

"Blueberry rakers can live anywhere."

The trailer park had lots of them, and they had a million kids that ran around loose, like dogs or cats. I liked the kids, though. Sometimes I performed for them. They sat in the dust around my front door and I stood on the stoop. I felt bad for the way they lived. I could remember hiding in the boot closet, making myself invisible, while my old man prowled the house looking for me, and I figured these kids had the same kind of stuff going on.

Bobby said, "I get the old blues myself, some-times."

"Bad?"

"Pretty bad."

"Bad enough so you start to think it isn't worth it?"

"I don't know about that," he said.

"How do you pull out of it?"

"It just happens."

"Like magic?"

"Like one of your tricks."

I swallowed some brandy and passed it to him. My ears were starting to ring a little. "The Sheriff thought I should jump off the bridge."

"Kind of radical."

"Works every time, though."

He shook his head, took a big drink. There was a little left, and he gave it to me. "Don't jump off the bridge," he said. Then he stood up. "I'm gonna call you in the morning."

I sighed.

"You'll be fine," he said. "Coffee brandy." He gave me a thumb's-up. There was a tap at my door just then, and his eyes widened. He turned his thumb over and followed it to the door. Typical Kincaid. It made me laugh in spite of myself.

Three little kids were crowded onto my stoop.

Here it was after midnight. I knew two of them: skinny Carlo and his sister, Eva, who never talked. They lived in the green trailer. A third kid, built like Carlo but with a tough little fighter's face, stood with them. I didn't know where he lived.

"Well?" Bobby said.

I leaned out from the couch, looking back at the kids. They weren't saying anything. I got very tired all of a sudden, waiting for them to speak. I was too buzzed for magic anyway. I said, "Sorry, not now," and fell back onto the sofa.

Bobby said, "Try him tomorrow. He's not feeling too good." They scampered off. He clicked the door shut and looked at me. "You're pathetic."

I reached for the last of the Sombrero.

"I'm calling you in the morning," he said. "Forget about jail. We've all been to jail. That ain't no excuse for nothing." He pointed a finger at me, and then he turned it over and followed it to the door.

I'd gone to jail for fighting one of the blueberry rakers at Country Rose's Bar and Grill. Rose had Karaoke every Friday night, and I'd taken to drinking there so I could listen. I liked it best when it was slow because the waitresses would go up onto the little stage, and I liked the angelic expressions they would get singing.

That Friday they had this busboy up on the stage, trying to get him to perform Wasted Days and Wasted Nights. He was a shy, chubby kid who couldn't keep his shirt tucked in and they were teasing him by making him sing, but in a nice way. His face was bright red, but he was happy about it and doing all right. Then this big, old raker with a voice like a bullfrog yelled, "I'm wasting tonight, listening to you!" from a table right behind me, and the busboy stopped singing.

"Ha!" the raker yelled out. "Get the waitress up there!"

He had a dirty denim vest on over his flannel shirt and a checked bandana around his neck. There were a couple of other guys sitting at the table, enjoying the ruckus.

The waitress told the busboy to ignore him, and he tried, but as soon as he opened his mouth again the blueberry raker yelled, "Get that fat kid off the stage!"

The kid shook his head then, and stepped down.

The blueberry raker clapped his hands loudly. His buddies crowed, and he looked around the room for more admirers. When our eyes met, he winked.

I threw what was left of my beer right into his smirk.

He sputtered and ran at me, and when I punched him in the face he sat right down on the floor. But he bounced up swinging and off we went. We took out tables and chairs, glass busting all over the place, and kept at it until the cruiser arrived with its siren whooping.

Bobby kept his promise, and let the phone ring and ring. I wrapped a pillow around my head. My brain was pounding and I couldn't remember going to bed. I felt like hell because I knew I wouldn't get back to sleep, and I'd have to lie there miserable, thinking about those kids, wondering what in the world was wrong with me.

The ringing stopped, finally.

I lay there in the dark and pictured the bridge, high over the narrow, rocky river. I took the pillow off my head and sat up. My windows were open, and as early and dark as it was, the smell of coffee was in the air, and a country western tune twanged faintly from the other side of the trailer park. It was blueberry rakers, ready to head for the barrens. A couple of driveways over a car started roughly. Someone kicked the idle down, put it in gear and drove it to the intersection. He headed off on Dearborne Road. A little later another car whooshed by.

It's a lonely sound: traffic before dawn.

I couldn't lie there listening to it. I went into my little tin box of a bathroom and did my business in the dark, then ran water in the sink and took six aspirin. Then I went into my little tin corner of a kitchen and had a cup of coffee by the light from the stove hood. I looked out the window at the kids' dark trailer and wondered what time the party had ended, and whether they'd managed to get any sleep.

I took another cup of coffee outside and sat on my front step. The stars were still out. Way down at the entrance to the trailer park a traffic light flashed. It was the only illumination in the park, since somebody had knocked out the last streetlight while I was in jail. I looked around, saw, off in the distance, the early Boston flight angling into the sky. I pictured Bobby swerving along the dark roads toward the airport, cussing me out for not answering the phone.

I sat back, lit a cigarette and drank my coffee. I looked around the trailer park and tried one more time to figure just how I'd come to this time and place. The Sheriff's fat face came into my mind and I remembered how disgusted he'd been, and how the kids had peered into the cage at me. I decided to finish my coffee and head on out to the bridge. I'd watch the sun come up, drop a few rocks and see what happened.

It had been a bummer to wake up sore and miserable again in jail. The bright lights had hurt my eyes. And it didn't help when the Sheriff came waddling down the corridor and said, "By God, you must love it here, Joe."

"Home sweet home," I said.

"How many times this year?"

"I don't keep track."

"Maybe you should." He took a damp washcloth out of a plastic bag and tossed it into the cell. "Clean yourself up," he said. "You've got company."

"Who?"

"Schoolboys," he said, and this smile crawled over his face. "Our annual tour. Usually it's kind of boring. It's much more interesting when we have a real, live asshole to put on display for them."

I sat up on the cot. "I don't want any kids looking at me."

"Too bad." He nodded at the washcloth. "You can use that, or sit there with blood on your face. I don't give a damn. It's up to you." He waited while I wiped my face and knuckles, then stuck the plastic bag between the bars and said, "Drop it in here. We wouldn't want you tearing it into strips and hanging yourself off the light fixture. Isn't that what you drunks like to do?"

He was some Sheriff.

I went over and dropped the washcloth into the bag. He twisted it shut and said, "Hey, I got a better idea, Joe. Don't hang yourself, jump off the bridge. Somebody does it every year; this might as well be your turn. It'll save me a hell of a lot of trouble. By the time they find you you'll be ten miles downriver and somebody else's problem."

"Anything for you," I said.

He shuffled off, laughing to himself. Five minutes later he brought the schoolboys back. That was an experience, sitting there as a living example of assholeness. The Sheriff told them that I liked to get drunk and fight, and that if they wanted to be like me they could look forward to enjoying the County's hospitality, too. He told them what it was like, the food, how much exercise you got, that sort of thing, and let them look into the cell.

They were typical eighth-grade boys.

Some were almost grown, with long hair and fuzzy mustaches, others still little kids. When it was time to go one of the bigger ones got brave and said, "Too bad you're not Houdini, huh?" and the rest of them glanced one last time into the cell and laughed nervously. I didn't say anything back. They were just being kids.

Slowly a red flush seeped along the horizon. A few more people knocked around in their trailers at the other end of the park. Another car started. It was still quiet at my end, though, quiet enough that when the door of green trailer banged open, I jumped a foot.

They came outside, the three of them, and stood rubbing their eyes. My first impulse was to tell them to go back to bed. I still didn't want to talk to anyone. But I'd already hurt their feelings once, so I stayed put. They didn't move, and after a minute I pointed at Carlo and said, "What's that on your PJs?"

Carlo looked down at himself. "Ducks," he said.

"Come show me?"

They walked across and stood in front of me, looking down at the ground, hands at their sides. There were rows of ducks swimming, ducks splashing, ducks waddling, on their pajamas. Nice," I said. "Listen, I'm sorry I was rude to you guys."

Carlo's bright eyes flickered up. "Okay."

"Eva?"

She gave me the briefest of looks.

"You know she don't talk," Carlo said.

"That's okay," I said. "She doesn't have to talk. Any girl with ducks on her PJs doesn't have to do anything she doesn't want to."

Eva turned away.

I looked at the third kid.

"Joaquin," Carlo said, and made a face. "You like that name?"

"Sure," I said. "That's a fine name."

Joaquin peered at me. He was wearing different PJs.

"He lives over there." Carlo pointed toward the far end of the trailer park, where the bushes came up close and where a row of privies had been built across a trench. It was funny: even a trailer park had its slums, in relative terms.

"Uh-huh," I said. "So, you come over for a trick?"

"Invisible ball!" Carlo said.

Eva turned back, her eyes as dark and shiny as polished chestnuts.

"I don't have a paper bag."

Carlo ripped one out of the hip pocket of his PJs.

I looked at it skeptically. "I don't know if my magic works on old, wrinkled-up lunch-bags."

"Aw, man..." Carlo said.

"Wait a minute," I said. "Don't give up the ship."

Carlo and Eva looked at each other. I stuck a hand in the bag, whacked it around. "It might work."

Carlo nudged Joaquin, who slapped at his arm.

I cracked my knuckles, made as if to pluck something out of thin air and quickly stuck it into my mouth. Then I moved my tongue around, figure-eighting it from cheek to cheek.

"That just his tongue!" Joaquin said.

"You wait!" Carlo concentrated on me.

I pulled the invisible ball out of my mouth, walked out into the lane and looked around. Then I flung it high into the ink-wash sky, and held the paper bag out. The ball fell into the bag with a satisfying snap.

"See!" Carlo said.

"Again!" Joaquin said.

I tossed it up again, this time crookedly so that I had to trot along the lane to catch it. Snap!

Carlo did a little scuff-step, clapped his hands.

I threw the ball higher and higher, circling under it like a catcher after a popup, the last dim stars spinning above me. Finally, going after a very high toss, I lost my balance and lurched sideways, staggering between two of the trailers, tripping and taking a heavily-laden clothesline down with me.

I sprawled on the warm grass, tangled in damp shirts, jeans and Holiday Inn towels. There was a wet towel over my face, and when I laughed, I could feel my own warm breath. I didn't move until the kids scampered up, and then I snaked an arm free, held the bag out and let the ball, airborne for a long time now, snap home.

"Caught it!" Carlo said.

Somebody, Joaquin, snatched the paper bag away. I heard him crinkling it, looking for the ball. Meanwhile I lay under the damp clothes. The grass was soft under me and the weight of the clothes sort of comforting. It

reminded me of the boots in the boot closet, when I was
a kid, hiding from the old man's temper. Then I felt
something gentle, a corner of the towel lifting, and
Eva's solemn face hung before me. She leaned closer.
Her eyes were shiny. I felt her breath, and then she
folded the towel all the way back, and I saw the sky
filling with oranges and reds.

The boys came up to help and quickly I was free
of the damp clothes. I swatted grass off my pants,
looked around to see if anybody was watching. The
trailers nearby were still dark, though. No blueberry
rakers there, or they'd already gone. I found the end of
the clothesline and held it up. The clothes were heavy. I
walked it back to the trailer and stretched the loop over
its rusted hook.

We all strolled back to my stoop.

I took the bag from Joaquin, dug the invisible ball
out and screwed it back into the air. "That's that," I said,
and dusted my hands together.

Joaquin frowned at me. "How you do that?"

"Can't tell you," I said. "Get in big trouble with the
Magician's Union."

"Another trick!" Carlo said.

So I went into my two-bit routine. I made coins
disappear and pulled them out of the kids' ears; I broke
my forefinger in two and put it back together. I went
inside for three Dixie Cups and three balls of cotton and
moved the balls through the cups without touching
them.

The kids, even Joaquin, laughed.

Eva didn't speak, but looked as if she might. I tried
to think of a trick so good she would have to say some-

thing, but before I could, a car peeled off from Dearborne and whistled around the corner toward us. It was a taxicab, trailing a cloud of dust, and Bobby Kincaid was driving, face crowded up close to the windshield, elbows stuck out to the side. The kids shrieked and flew back across the street. I laughed at them running in their PJs. They scurried up the steps and into their trailer. The taxi skidded to a stop, and Bobby shoved the door open.

"It lives," he said.

"It wanted to sleep," I said. "But somebody wouldn't let it."

"Get in," he said.

I slumped into the front seat and shut the door. He pulled a U-turn and headed toward the intersection. We slid around the corner onto Dearborne, and about a mile along stopped for coffee and jelly donuts. Then we left town, riding out past the barrens, where hunched people in silhouette rhythmically swept the hilltops with their blueberry rakes.

The sun was up when we started across the Bucksport bridge. I looked out the window at the water far below. The tide had come up the river, covering the rocks. As we passed gulls jumped off the railings and wheeled underneath the bridge, catching the breeze, looking clean and white as angels in the new morning sunlight.

We ramped off the bridge and followed the road around a curve into the woods. In twenty minutes we were cruising down avenues lined with oaks, through squares with brick office buildings. At the taxi shack I signed out my car and followed Bobby to the airport.

We parked at the cabstand by the Delta Airlines gate.
He slammed his door and walked back, and we leaned
on my cab to wait for the first flight.

"Nice morning," Bobby said.

"Not bad," I said.

The airport came slowly to life. A half-dozen flight
attendants got out of a Ramada Inn van and pulled their
little wheeled bags into the building. The maintenance
crew was sweeping, cleaning. Hertz girls arrived for
work, crossing the parking lot toward the terminal,
wearing their bumblebee dresses. One of them even
gave us a smile before she went inside.

"What do you think of that?" Bobby said.

"Sweet."

He raised his coffee cup and I reached over and
tapped mine against it. It was a nice morning. I didn't
feel all that bad for a sorry son of a bitch with a hangover who'd been a jail exhibit for schoolboys.

I leaned back against the taxi and shut my eyes. It
was the trailer-park kids, I knew. Their sleepy eyes, the
ducks on their PJs, the way they could still believe in
magic. It was Eva, especially. Next time I would get her
to talk. Meanwhile I would remember the way she had
looked at me, her sweet breath on my cheek. And how
she had swept the towel off my face, dramatically, like
a real magician, and then had stepped aside to let the
morning fill with light.

The Dilly

I WAS stupid for a long time, I admit it. But then I smartened up, and as soon as our gig with the light-house was done, I jumped in my pickup and headed north. I was going to drive all night. It seemed impor-tant to get there before Sweeney went to work in the morning. I didn't want to cover eight hundred miles only to miss her by ten minutes. Besides, what if today was the day she was supposed to meet Mr. Right?

You know.

I could picture Sweeney in her kitchen, me walk-ing in. She'd be poking around, getting some breakfast, or maybe just toast and coffee: she'd never had much use for breakfast until I moved in. I changed that habit and a few others. Living alone, for instance. She'd lived by herself, up in the woods, next to the lake. She'd never had any problem living alone, until I came around.

It was pitch dark out, and so cold the stars seemed
shrunken in the sky. I fed the pickup a little more gas,
watched the needle swing across the grass-green numbers. There wasn't much traffic. A couple of cars slid by.
After an hour or two I caught up to a tractor-trailer, old
but in good shape, cruising like a battleship, lit up in
orange and red. He was going at a good clip and I
settled in behind him.

Most of the work we did on the lighthouses was
cosmetic. Painting, patching, repairing the docks and
what-have-you. Your basic upkeep. But in Maine, and
then at this town on Chesapeake Bay, we had to re-wire
the beacons. The lights went out and when the boys
from the bases looked into it, they found rotting old
wiring and connections.

So in we came to make it right.

We spent six months in Maine and then went down
to this town on Pocomoke Sound for another six
months. These weren't jobs you finished in a week or
two. You were there long enough to become part of
things. In Maryland, they even had a goodbye party to
thank us for fixing their lighthouse. The Mayor orga-
nized it. You would have thought we were family. They
had these perky Sea Princesses from the Crab festival
there.

It had been different in Maine.

Only one girl saw me off there, and she was in
tears.

I met Sweeney at the Coast Guard open house.
They have one every summer in Rockland. I was a host,

in dress blues, and Sweeney talked to me for an hour. Later we went dancing, had a few drinks, ended up at her place, a log-cabin house on a hill over Seven Tree Pond. I stayed over, we hung out the next day and, well, you know how that goes.

I spent the rest of my time there with her. We covered a lot of territory. She liked fishing, even. At night we would slide Sweeney's canoe out onto the lake, crack a six-pack and drop a line.

We burned deadfall wood on her little beach in the dark.

So why did I launch? It was standard procedure. Half the fun of being in the Coast Guard was seeing new places, meeting new women. We all did it. It was competitive, even, to see who found a place to live fastest. And we were in the habit of leaving them behind.

They were just girls.

But Sweeney was different. Maybe I didn't realize it right away. But give me credit for finally catching on. And, after it happened, for jumping in my old pickup, for heading back as fast as I could go.

I fiddled with the radio, picking up talk shows. They all had a guest who thought he had something figured out. This one was talking about hurricanes. He said they were caused by negative ions from all the humans on the surface of the earth. He thought these bad ions were messing up winds and barometric pressure.

Sure, I thought. Why not?

Later a guy explained all about the UFO sightings.

I drove along, listening. There wasn't much traffic and the sky was dark and the stars led me on until I got into Connecticut, and then I could see light reflecting off a blanket of low clouds. I moved farther under the clouds. Soon the sky had disappeared completely. I rolled down the window and it was colder and I rolled the window back up. I switched the radio off, wished for a CB so I could talk to the driver of the tractor-trailer up ahead. From the way he switched lanes I thought he was probably a decent guy. He drove fast, but careful. He used his blinkers. The rig banged over bumps as if it were empty, and I thought he was probably heading home. Then I started to wonder about his wife. When he got within range he would give her a call on the CB. I pictured her in her nightgown, talking to him. Her hair would be up with a little strand fallen free. She would smell like warm flannel. She would hold the microphone against her cheek. When he signed off, she would look at the mike and then kiss it.

Breaker, breaker.

I followed the tractor-trailer around a high hill. There were houses on the hill, all their windows dark. Then we were past the hill and the land sloped down to meet us and we were rolling through a flat plain. I tried to figure how far away from Maryland I was, how much closer to Maine. I thought about how long I'd been away, without writing or calling, how long I'd been stupid in Maryland, before I saw the light.

You know politicians, always looking for an angle. The Mayor in Maryland was like that, and when we finished with the repair, he decided it was a great

chance for a little publicity. He tied it in with this old
tragedy, a whaler that had gone down on its maiden
voyage in 1875. The connection was that it had been
the last ship launched before the lighthouse was com-
pleted. I thought that was a stretch, since the ship sank
off Newfoundland. I don't know what difference a
beacon in Maryland would have made. But he didn't let
that stand in his way. He got the council to go along and
on the big day most of the town was assembled on the
main dock and the overflow covered the smaller docks
nearby. The Mayor had the Sea Princesses in their little
green outfits. He had a couple trumpets, a trombone, a
tuba from the high school band. They played the Star
Spangled Banner while the Mayor saluted the flagpole
on the roof of one of the shacks. Then he pointed to the
lighthouse, sitting on a rock out in the bay. He gave a
signal and somebody out there threw a switch and the
light came on and started rotating. The Sea Princesses
skipped around cheering and clapping.

It was cold, breezy there on the docks.

These crab boats that had been waiting took off,
lug-lugging through the harbor, picking their way back
to work. They'd just wanted to see that the light was
really repaired.

The Mayor was talking about the tragedy.

You could see his breath in the air.

I stood by with the rest of the crew. We were at
attention. But we weren't paying attention. We already
knew the story. At our rehearsal the Mayor had passed
out photocopies of old news articles about it. The ship
had been called the Dilly, and she was a four-masted
whaler. There was a tintype that showed everybody

gathered at the landing to send her off. They gave the Captain a silver dollar for good luck and his wife kissed him goodbye and they put him in a tender and rowed him out to the ship, where he nailed the coin to the mast.

Some coin.

Some good luck.

They raised the sails and the boys all waved goodbye and everybody on the shore waved back and the ship blew slowly out of sight down the bay, heading for the ocean, and that was the last anyone saw of them.

They gave us a medallion at the Mayor's ceremony, a gold-plated coin about as big as a Susan B. Anthony dollar. There was a lighthouse stamped on it, and streams of light coming out of the beacon, shining over a rocky shore. There was a little seagull flying over the rocks. The coin had a hole in it where you could thread a necklace.

I'd expected something ordinary.

But this had been nice enough to give to Sweeney. I looked at it on the dashboard and thought about what she might say to me. I'd caught up with the tractor-trailer again, and I followed him along the highway, over the soft rolling contours of the land, rehearsing my arrival. I wondered if the tractor-trailer driver's wife made it a point to be awake when he got home, if she made love to him no matter what time it was. Somehow I thought that she was that kind of wife. Then I wondered if I'd be as lucky, if we'd both have our women, their warm bodies, their sweet eyes.

Many of the Dilly's crew had been married, and in one of the newspaper stories they'd listed the name of every widow, starting with the captain's wife, whose name was Millicent. This didn't happen until two years after they'd left port, because it took that long for the town to believe they'd been lost. They must have begun to wonder after a few months, when no word had come as to how they were doing. But those whaling trips took years. The wives were used to waiting, and would have let themselves hope for quite a while. But eventually they knew the truth. Maybe another ship found some debris, a lifeboat or something. I don't know. But the newspaper listed them as dead, and their wives as widows. The whole front page was devoted to them. Town businesses bought black-bordered ads that had prayers for the souls of the lost sailors.

The Mayor went through the whole story. Then he said something I didn't know, and that was how Millicent, the Captain's wife, on the anniversary of the Dilly's departure, came down to the landing and dropped a wreath on the outgoing tide. Millicent didn't made a big deal about it, but a few people noticed. The next year she did it again and more of the townfolk were present. Then every year they gathered on the big town dock and dropped a wreath. Millicent took part until her death in 1915.

I figured in my head: thirty-nine years.

After she died they dropped the wreath without her a couple of times, but then came WWI and that was the end of it.

"Until now," the Mayor said.

He stepped back from the podium and the Sea

Princesses walked to the edge of the dock and dropped a big evergreen wreath down into the water, and all the spectators crowded over to watch the outgoing tide pull it up and over the choppy little waves. The Sea Princesses skipped back to their places behind the podium. The wreath floated away, smaller all the time, until I couldn't see it. I wanted to turn my head. But I was still at attention.

The Mayor said a little prayer and thanked everyone for coming.

Then we all spent some time mingling with the townspeople, shaking hands. I was still trying to watch the wreath, though. I just couldn't get over Millicent. I thought that the Captain of the Dilly must have been quite a guy to have a woman love him so, and I wondered if anyone would ever love me that much. Then I remembered Sweeney crying when I left. I'd shut the door and walked out onto her porch and I could still hear her sobs. But I'd kept going. Can you believe it?

From below I could hear the salt water washing against the stonework. The light was flashing out there on the rock. The wreath got smaller and smaller and there was a cold breeze in my face.

That night I headed north.

It was four o'clock when I crossed the Piscataqua River into Maine. I made a quick stop at the food-and-gas place on the turnpike for coffee. Then I took off again. The tractor-trailer was still in front of me, an old friend by now. Every time I passed him on a rise, he blinked his high beams to let me know when to cut back in. Then, on the downside, when he roared past, I did the same. He'd swing into the lane in front of me and set his running lights blinking in a pattern.

He took the bypass at Brunswick, and gave me a blast on the air horn when he saw I wasn't following. I tooted and rushed on, following Route 1 through the small towns, making good time because it was still early. In another hour I was driving through Rockland, where all the buildings have false third floors, like a frontier village. There was the ferry terminal, where Sweeney and I had boarded a day-trip out to Vinalhaven Island. We'd had a picnic on a cliff overlooking the ocean. The ferry was tied up at its slip. Past it I could see the deep-water harbor with its long breakwater and another old lighthouse I'd helped repair.

I drove on through town, imagining what would happen. My heart was thumping. I'd give her the medallion and tell her what a fool I'd been. Then I'd take her into my arms.

I headed out into the country.

I drove alongside Seven Tree Pond for a mile and turned down the fire road that led to Sweeney's. It had been a hard winter on the dirt road, which was ribbed and pot-holed, not smooth the way I remembered. It wasn't dawn yet, but off to my left I could see pieces of the lake flickering through the barren trees. Then the water came up close to the road and I saw the end of Sweeney's long driveway. She had a new mailbox, made to look like her log-cabin, and as I approached it felt like coming home. My eyes got a little wet and I had to blink. I turned off the fire road, crested a little

rise in her driveway and there was the house, dark
upstairs but with a light on in the kitchen.

I hit the brakes, skidded to a stop.

Sweeney's Toyota sat at the top of the driveway,
and a brand-new eighteen-wheeler was parked to the
right of her porch steps. You could tell from the tracks
in the grass that it wasn't the first time. It looked comfortable, as if it belonged. I sat there for a minute,
letting it sink in, and then I rammed the pickup into
reverse and backed out the way I'd come, stopping by
the mailbox to read:

Sweeney/Jacobs.

The Sanderson lighthouse stands at the end of a
mile-long breakwater. I walked out, looking at the open
ocean, thinking about the Dilly, wondering what had
happened out there a hundred years ago. Had they
ignored signs of bad weather, chasing whales maybe,
hoping to beat a coming storm? Did they pass too close
to an iceberg? Who could say. Most likely mistakes
were made, though. Maybe only one mistake.

Sometimes that's enough.

I sat down on one of the slatted benches next to the
lighthouse. The turret had marks we'd left behind.
Every lighthouse has them, where they've been worked
on. They're like fingerprints. You don't notice them
unless you've been involved with one.

I looked at my watch.

Sweeney would be running around, trying not to
forget anything, gulping coffee, looking for her boots.
"Who was that in the driveway?" she might ask her Mr.
Jacobs. He'd tell her it was just some guy turning

around. People got lost all the time on those fire roads.

I sat there until morning came. When I scaled the medallion out into the harbor it sparkled in the sunlight. Then there was a little splash and for just a moment I saw it winking down through the water.

C'est La Vie

Listen: I was a quarterback from the time I was twelve right up through my freshman year at college, the whole time living for that moment when you stroll up behind the center with the game on the line and the coaches watching and the spectators yelling and everybody waiting for you to set things in motion.

This was my life, n'est-ce pas?

All right.

But then I blow out a knee during summer practice. I'm done for the year and maybe for good, depending on how I recover from the surgery. I'm under the knife for four hours, and they do a number that will let me play again if it works, but if it doesn't I'll need another and my playing days will be over.

Nice.

Back at school, they take away my tutors because I'm inactive. And I've never been much with the books.

I last a few weeks, crutching around campus, then quit because I can see what's coming: I'll flunk out for sure, which will make it harder to come back the next fall, when theoretically the knee will be recovered.

Okay.

I load up the Belair and head home. The old jalopy doesn't deal well with hills and when I get to the mountains it slows down to a crawl. It takes four hours and when I finally pull in the driveway beside the old man's pickup my knee, just out of the cast, is aching like a son of a bitch.

The old lady comes out onto the porch. She stands there in her curlers and pink corduroys, looking eager, wanting to hug and kiss, but I tell her I'm in no mood and besides I've got to unpack, and I start lugging things into the house, limping you know, and after a while she swallows her disappointment--she wanted me to cry on her shoulder--and pitches in and then the old man tears himself away from the TV long enough to clap me on the back and help, too.

Pretty soon I'm re-installed in my room. I look around at the pennants, pictures of teams, footballs with dates and scores. There are trophies all over the place, a bookcase with more awards than books. On my desk is a big album of clippings that my mother saved for me over the years, and I open the album to the last page, where the two most recent articles are waiting to be arranged inside the plastic.

One has the headline: JOEY CLOUTIER SUF-FERS KNEE INJURY.

The last one is a little stiffer, as if I'm already half-forgotten. CLOUTIER LEAVES SCHOOL, it says.

So I'm home. I do the rehab exercises in the
morning, working hard enough to make the room stink,
even though I open the river-side window and let the
cool breeze blow in. Then after lunch I have to get out
of the house and I jump in the car and cruise up and
down the streets. The town seems smaller than before,
the houses shabbier. It's just a little French town. I cross
the steel bridge over the river and ride around the
country looking at the farms, and then come back. The
Belair struggles along: there's no compression left and
it stalls a lot, but keeps going. I know it should be
looked at but I'd have to take it to Jerry's Sunoco out on
Mast Road and sit around half the day waiting, and it's
just too much to think of.

You know how it is.

Then one afternoon it won't move out of the
driveway. It starts all right, but as soon as I put it in
gear stalls. I sit there looking out at the dead leaves
blowing around the yard, a little afraid to try it again,
because this could be it with the old car, and I don't
want to know that. But finally I try it again.

It stalls.

I keep trying, lurching a few feet toward the street
each time. Eventually I'm so pissed I floor it until the
engine is roaring. I'm beating on the steering wheel,
daring it to stall again. Without letting up on the gas I
throw it into drive, and there's a metallic screech and a
bang loud enough to bring Mrs. Rioux to her door
across the street. She looks out at me, shakes her head,
then goes back inside and shuts the door. I sit there in
the dead car.

Smoke's seeping up from the hood.

I'm fuming, too.

It was a stupid no-contact drill, the kind you have so you won't get injuries. No helmets, pads, nothing. I was rolling out and Jimmy Evans--a tight end filling in on defense for this drill, getting into the role, pretending to be a bad-ass--thought he'd be cute and chase me. I can see him running after me, dirt flying up from his spikes. He laughed and grabbed my shirt like he was going to slam-dunk me: big joke. Only my foot was caught in a field drain. When I screamed Jimmy lowered me to the ground. I pulled my knee up tight against my chest. I could smell the turf and hear Coach's feet thudding as he ran out from the bench.

He bent to look at me, then straightened and slapped Jimmy's face, hard. Jimmy stood there and took it, kept saying he was sorry. The trainer pushed him out of the way and knelt down to pry my hands loose; he manipulated the joint until I let out another holler. Then he looked up at Coach.

"Well?" Coach said.

"It's not good."

Coach swore and then he and the trainer carried me over to Coach's Town and Country and loaded me in and took me to the hospital. We drove around the track to get to the exit and all the kids stood on the field, watching, holding their helmets by the faceguards.

Let me tell you about knee surgery: it's to be avoided if at all possible.

The old man hauls the Belair to his brother's junkyard across the river and then gets me a job ironing shoes in the shoeshop. Just till I'm better, he says. I've never had to work there, unlike most of the people in town, but I know everybody anyway: it's Mike Cote, my favorite receiver during high school, who shows me how to iron.

"See these?" Mike says that first day, holding out his arm. "The iron gets slippery. You got to watch it."

I look out the grimy window at the rows of old cars, their windshields glinting in the sun. "I'll be careful," I say. But I've got welts, too, before the week is out. The problem is you have to concentrate, and I keep daydreaming. I think about my senior year, when they let the whole shoeshop out early, so nobody would have to miss the trip north for the State Championship game. We had a caravan of townies following our bus. The cheerleaders rode with us and chanted the whole way. Debbie Wilkinson sat in my lap and kissed me and the coaches just laughed about it. I remember the thick feel of her sweater. All the townies were drinking beer in their pickups and by the time we got to Presque Isle half of them were shitfaced, and during the game there were fights in the stands. The next night, back in town, there was a parade down Main Street under the elms with me in the high seat on the lead firetruck. There were guys from the shop all along the street cheering, some of them with black eyes, the same guys I was working with now.

After a while I start bringing my football to work, and at lunchtime Mike and I go outside and throw it back and forth. I can't move much because of the knee, but there's nothing wrong with my arm. I throw one, and Mike runs after it and catches it. He takes a couple of hops and stretches back and throws it hard. It lands short and skips sideways and I limp over to the railroad berm and bend like a stork to pick it up. It's dusty out there: the fall has been dry and warm this year.

"Hey, remember what they called us?" Mike says.

"The French Connection." I throw one as hard as I can. Mike laughs, sprints to reach up and make a nice catch. Then he runs in a leaning half-circle, nonchalant, dropping the football behind him, as if scoring yet another touchdown.

At quarter to one, we sit down in the shade of the south wing to eat lunch. Mike eats half of his sandwich in one bite and chews with his cheek sticking out and his mouth open. I'm a little embarrassed to be back where people eat like that.

"Look at the old man," I say. He's playing volleyball and his gut is bouncing under the t-shirt he always wears. Dust puffs up from his feet. He jumps and hits the ball with his fist; it goes into the net.

"They play evenings at the high school," Mike says.

"I heard." I make a furrow in the dirt with the heel of my sneaker.

"I'm thinking of helping them out."

I feel my knee. The clicking and rubbing has stopped, but it's still stiff as hell and sometimes when I move just right there's this tremendous pop. It's taking a long time to come around.

"Christ, I couldn't even play volleyball now," I say.

"Maybe when it's all better."

"Then I won't want to."

"How's it coming, anyway?"

"All right," I say.

"Well, I wish you luck." Mike washes down his sandwich with coffee.

The whistle on the roof blows, and my old man walks over, his face red as an apple, drops of sweat popping out on his forehead. He wipes his face on his t-shirt and I look away from his sweaty old gut.

"Il f'chaud," he gasps. "Hooo!"

"It ain't hot," I say.

"Sure, not to stand there and throw-throw-throw. Why don't you play with us?"

"For one thing," I say, "I can't jump."

He can't quite believe in knee injuries, and he snorts a little. The whistle blows again and we all head for the enclosed stairway that's stuck to the side of the building. It's like a dark tunnel and we climb up to the third floor where it's hot as hell and the machines are just starting to clatter across the wide, open room.

Mike and I head off for the irons and my old man waves and crosses the floor to his tacker and switches it on. He slips right into the old piece-work dance. There are five of them in a row in their t-shirts and jeans, walking in place, moving all over, grabbing shoes off the racks and slapping them in the holders, turning them this way and that, moving at the same time, like a good backfield.

Mike and I are on the clock. We punch in by the foreman's office and walk past Denis Archambeau in his foul-weather gear, hobbling around and around the soaking tub, poking the shoes with a mop handle, rubbing his big hook-nose. He's got something wrong with him that makes him knock-kneed, but he gets around pretty well anyway. He's my old man's age and I can remember him since I was a kid. He's always been crazy. Nobody knows if it's from breathing the fumes or if he was born that way, but one sign of his craziness is you can't leave anything lying around or he'll steal it. He steals things and you never get them back. He stole Mike Cote's letter jacket out of the pool hall once and Mike and I followed him across the bridge to his house but his mother answered the door and wouldn't let us in, she jabbered French at us until we left. She had bright red spots on her cheeks. She was as crazy as Denis so maybe it ran in the family and wasn't the fumes.

As I'm watching Denis work one of the embossers across the room, Mike throws a handful of tacks at him and the tacks rattle off his slicker onto the floor.

Denis tips his head back and laughs: "Ha-ha!"

"Listen to it," Mike says. He's never forgiven Denis for stealing that jacket.

We go to the irons and I take the left shoe of a pair off the slant-shelved rack and press it against the iron. The iron is shaped like an on-end prism. The shoe's just leather attached to a wooden mold at this point, and as I lean on it steam rises and the wrinkles begin to vanish. I have to be careful not to sear the leather. It's hot on the third floor and sweat drips off my nose and spatters on the iron.

I do the other shoe. When the rack is done I push it over to an embosser. It's hard to push straight because the casters are bent. I get another rack from Denis Archambeau and work it past Mike to my station.

Denis laughs at me and Mike shakes his head.

I'm thinking: What a strange place, and now here I am with them. But not for long, I hope. This is just a temporary situation. Meanwhile I try to hide how it makes me feel.

I try to hide it at home, too, because whenever the old lady thinks I'm down she wants me to pray with her.

"The hell with that," I say finally.

"Don't turn away from the Lord, Joey." She's just come back from the hairdresser's with a full, kinky perm, the kind you see on a diner waitress, which is what my mother is. She has to go in to work and she's wearing the blue uniform that makes her look like an old cheerleader.

"Spare me," I say. We're in the living room watching the tube. They're televising the school's games this year and every Saturday I sit there and watch the kid who replaced me get better and better, which doesn't improve my disposition. I've been crabbing and bitching about my injury, which is why the old lady started in.

"The Lord will help you," the old lady says. "But first you have to ask him."

"I'll help myself."

"He'll be fine when he's back in school," my old man says from the couch.

"You shut up," the old lady says.

"Throw the ball!" the old man yells.

"He didn't have anyone open," I say.

"He coulda thrown it away."

The old lady glares at both of us, then gives up and heads off to work.

We watch the whole game. It's tough to sit still,

though, for that length of time, because I'm full of the old butterflies. Inside I still think I'm going to play, and I get all juiced up and then have nothing to do with it. I hit the rehab work extra hard on Saturdays and that helps a little. But by game time I'm antsy. I've always been that way. It used to start the night before, and got to be a town joke: every Friday night Joey Cloutier would have to go out and walk. I'd walk all over the damn town, down Water Street past the shop, across the open stretch beside the river, past Roland's Bar and Grill, up the hill to the Catholic Church and the cemetery and down the other side to where the river curves around to the south and where the downtown starts. There'd always be somebody in Roland's or downtown who would yell out at me: "Gonna beat 'em tomorrow?"

"Gonna try," I'd yell back. Then I'd keep on walking. Somebody else would wish me luck. They all knew I was gearing myself up.

Everybody still goes to Roland's after work on Fridays. Mike and I are usually the first ones there, though, because we don't take part in the crap games that run on each floor of the shop. Then when the gamblers show up we try to guess who's won or lost by looking at their faces. It's easy enough: the games are cut-throat and people lose big money. Denis Archambeau isn't allowed to play anymore, because one Friday he lost his whole paycheck and the next Monday his old Memere marched in and raised hell with the foreman until he took up a collection to pay Denis back. But then they banned him. He still stands around watching, rubbing his nose, banging his knees together.

Every Friday Mike and I laugh at him and go down the stairway and out into the sunshine, feeling virtuous, and we scuff through the chestnut leaves along the river, tossing the football back and forth, walking through the shadows of the frame houses and then across the open stretch beside the river where it's always windy. I'm walking better, although I still can't run. Mike does all the running. He makes one last cut and I hit him by the door to the bar and he ducks through the doorway with both arms around the ball, like he's pounding it in from the one.

So fall slips by. The days get colder, and as December comes the snow holds off, but I can feel it in the breeze that whips down off the hills and across the river. It makes my knee ache where they cut into it. It's cold enough that they stop playing volleyball, but Mike and I still throw the football in the lee of the south wing. It gets too cold finally on Water Street though, and one Friday on the way to Roland's Mike says he's had enough, and we walk over without throwing the ball, with our collars up and shoulders hunched against the wind. We're the first to arrive, and take our normal seats at the middle of the bar.

Rollie Pelletier comes over, looking sleepy. He likes to doze in a chair by the woodstove when it's slow. I toss him the ball, he catches it easily and flips it back: at the high school there's a whole shelf of trophies from his era.

"What'll it be, boys?"

I set the football on the floor. Mike tells Rollie two draughts, and he walks down to the taps, moving under the wall-mounted TV. He brings the beer back.

I take a nice, cold drink, set the beer down and look at Mike.

"Good stuff." Mike pulls out his cigarette pack and offers it. I take one and lean toward his lighter: I've begun smoking a little but haven't taken up buying them yet.

Pop wipes down the bar and dries his hands on his apron. He asks us how things are going at the shop. Then he says, "How's that Archambeau?"

"Looney as ever."

"His mother," Rollie says. "She was a good-looking woman." He says it in French: "Sa Mere, elle etait une femme jolie." Then he gets this dreamy look on his face and keeps wiping his hands.

Mike winks at me. "Ever put the boots to her, Rollie?"

"I don't like that kind of talk," Rollie says, and stalks off to the other end of the bar and looks up at the TV. We snicker, drink our beers, wait for the rest of them to show, which they do before long: some happy, others trying to figure how much money they have left to drink on.

My old man marches in, waves a fistful of money.

"Joey!" he yells. "Want a drink? How about you, Mikey?"

"Sure, if you're buying," Mike says.

"Give the boys one," the old man tells Rollie. Then he puts his arm around me and kisses my cheek. He's been drinking already, and Rollie squints at him before he starts pouring. The old man's wearing a t-shirt under his biker's jacket and when he lifts his arm a smell comes off him.

"For chrissake, Pa," I say, and wipe my cheek with a sleeve.

The old man laughs, turns to Rollie and says, "Ca va?"

"Pas mal," Rollie grumps. He gives Mike and me a beer.

The old man slaps our backs and goes to join the rest of them around the pool table. Somebody pushes the coin slot in and the numbered balls roll through the machine, down to the vent and are plucked out and racked.

"Your old man was winner," Mike notes.

I nod.

We take a few turns at the table, losing every time to the older guys who, like my father, keep their own two-piece cues in cases behind the bar. Denis Archambeau tries to play and when they won't let him he starts banging on a pinball machine and Rollie has to yell at him. Then Denis sits down at the bar to sulk.

Later on my old man asks Rollie to turn on the game.

Rollie walks down to the channel control and starts clicking through the stations. It's a Friday night game. He turns up the sound and you can hear the crowd noise. The announcer is talking about the first half, pretending he knows about football, although he looks more like a golfer. Anyway he tells about all the scoring in the first half. Then the second half starts out the same way. The teams trade touchdowns. My replacement, this kid, is scrambling around, somehow keeping up with the other team's offense, which is smooth and efficient. Everybody in Roland's is watching. Every time we score there's a loud cheer.

It all comes down to a fourth-and-goal, and the kid walks up to the center like he knows he's going to do it, and then he does it, skipping away from a couple of tacklers and rifling a pass to Jimmy Evans in the end zone. Jimmy dives and catches it. He scrambles up, looks at the ref for the touchdown signal, holds the football up high in celebration. His teammates swarm over him. The kid quarterback jumps up and down, pumps his fist and runs past the other team's players, who are trudging off the field with their heads down.

In Roland's, everybody's going crazy.

The old man comes over and pats me on the back and says something about it being my turn after my leg's all better--he talks fast and in French so I don't catch it all--and I just nod.

"You ain't had any luck," he says.

"C'est la vie," I say, and drink off my beer.

On the screen, they're interviewing the kid. He's got black smudges under his eyes. Jimmy Evans is standing beside him, grinning, still holding the football. I slide off my stool and limp to the men's room. The old knee gives a pop when I step up to the urinal. I say, "That's enough out of you," and laugh, but I'm down. I know I'll never be able to run around like that again.

The rehab's not working.

I'm going to need that second operation.

I take a long time, come out to see everyone gathered around the pool table watching the old man run out a rack. I step up beside Mike to watch, too. The old man runs a hand through his hair, sights along the stick and banks the six into a corner pocket, leaving the cue ball close to the eight. He taps it in and cheers, punching the air.

Mike and I go back to the bar and I pull out my stool and look down at the bare floor.

"Hey," I say.

Mike looks. "It was right there."

Rollie points at the door. "I just saw that Archambeau sneaking out."

I move as fast as I can to the door and push it open.

It's dark out, windy, stiff leaves rattling over the ground. A car rolls by and turns toward the bridge and its lights fall on Denis Archambeau, knock-kneed as hell, hustling along with my football up against his chest.

"Look at it go," Mike says.

The car passes Denis and its tires hum as it crosses the river. Something snaps in me and I take off after him, so angry my knee doesn't even hurt at first, although it's clicking and popping like mad after the first few strides. By the time I reach the bridge it hurts, all right, but I just push harder. The more it hurts the more I force out of it. I've had it. I can hear Denis's feet making the metal of the bridge ring, and I start across after him.

What a sight we must be: Denis lurching along with his knees banging together, me following in a strange, one-sided gallop. I almost catch him, too. But then my knee locks up and I have to stop.

Denis keeps hobbling, crosses the river, heads off for home.

"Get back here!" I yell after him.

He ignores me. Pretty soon he's gone.

So all right.

I lean on the metal railing, look down at the water. The railing is cold. The water runs swiftly under the bridge and boils through a narrows to the curve that takes it out of town. There are big boulders in the bed of the river. I can't move and I stand there holding onto the railing until the old man's pickup stops, and then I hop to the door and climb in. He looks down at my leg, and for a moment I'm afraid he's going to try and make me feel better. But he doesn't say anything. He just puts it in gear and takes me home.

Giant

I was hoping he'd forget how angry he was with me, that it would be a kind of adventure for him to stay over. But not my Ricky. He wasn't ready to have a good time with his delinquent Dad. He didn't want it to be okay that I'd moved out. He wouldn't even shoot a game of eight-ball before we went upstairs.

"It stinks in here," he said. "Cigarettes, yuck!"

I shushed him. Rollie was listening from the bar and I didn't want to hurt his feelings when he'd been nice enough to open the apartment back up after swearing that he'd never have tenants again. I'd been crying in my beer about my wife, wondering where I'd go, and he'd just up and offered the place. It was pretty good of him.

I rolled my eyes at him and hustled Ricky through the pool hall and up the stairs. I got him a popsicle, took him into the little living room and sat him down. "That wasn't very polite," I said.

"Smoking's bad." He took a huge bite of the popsicle and opened the paperback he'd been carrying around with him. A great reader, old Ricky. This one was a schoolbook, but you'd have thought it was a Christmas gift. I leaned over and looked at the cover.

"Hey, I remember that when I was your age."

He looked at me like he didn't believe I was ever nine years old.

"I liked those Lilli-whatevers."

"Putians," Ricky said.

"Yeah, those guys."

He made a grim little face and held the book closer.

"So what do you want to do?" I said.

"Go home."

"C'mon, Ricky, you just got here."

"I mean both of us! Mummy said she was sorry."

"I know she did."

"Then why can't you come home?"

"It's complicated."

"You could if you wanted to."

"It's a grownup thing," I said.

It had been my wife's old boyfriend, which made it worse because he not only knew his way around her body, he was everything I wasn't. You know, tall dark and surly, someone who rode around on a motorcycle and didn't believe in jobs. While I was an inch taller than Suzy and made my living shuffling paper around in an office at the Sanderson Shoe Corp. I mean, I had aspirations, but that was where I was at the time.

I'd never quite figured why she'd chosen me over him in the first place, to tell you the truth, and to drive by the house one afternoon and spot his Harley tucked a little carelessly behind the garage; to walk back and peer in the living room window at Suzy with her arms at her sides and her eyes closed while he nuzzled her neck; well, let's just say the old doubts came roaring back as powerfully as ever.

I watched in a sick sort of trance until she felt me staring and her eyes opened and then widened, her face bloomed red and she pushed him away. Then I turned around and walked off.

She came running out after me, but I kept those little legs moving. Not exactly John Wayne striding off to war, you understand, but I managed to get to my car and leave her standing in tears on the road, and there was some small satisfaction in that.

Our only contact since had been my call to ask if Ricky could visit, and I'd kept that clinically brief, ignoring her attempts to apologize and explain until she'd given up. "All right, Ned. I'll drop him off."

"I'll pick him up after school. Just let him know, if you'd be so kind," I'd said, and hung up the phone.

I fired up a big, juicy hamburger and smothered it with ketchup and relish and cheese. I gave him half a gallon of Death By Chocolate ice cream for desert. And still he wouldn't cut me any slack. He didn't want to go to a movie. He didn't want to go bowling. He didn't want to go fishing.

"Stop looking at me!" he said.

"I'm bored."

"Then pick up! It's messy in here!"

I sighed and started moving around the apartment, picking up magazines, newspapers and dirty clothes. On one of the front pages I saw the article about the Russians.

I went back and said, "Got it!"

He blinked real slow.

"We'll rent a boat and take it down the river," I said. "There's a big Russian ship. It's only going to be here for another week. We'll go by and wave to them."

"Humph," Ricky said. But he lowered the book a little.

"You can steer," I said.

He put the book on his lap.

"Maybe we'll get a souvenir."

"Like what?" he said. "Old shoes, maybe? Dead fish?" But when I handed him his jacket, he came along all right.

It was about fifteen miles downriver to the bay. Ricky handled the throttle and we putted along past farms and cornfields, stretches of forest and a couple of little villages with bridges. It was cool but not cold and the light was nice, slanting over the tree tops. After an hour or so we popped out into the bay. I took the throttle then. "You did a great job," I said.

He turned away so I wouldn't see his pleasure.

The Russian ship sat low out beyond the breakwater. Crew members stood along the rail, high above the concave hull. Rust stained the metal below the anchor ports. We rode out close and started around the bow.

"Wave," I told Ricky.

He lifted his hand an inch. The men grinned at us.
One pointed toward the stern and started off, and as I
took the little boat in toward him we looked up at huge,
red, Cyrillic letters.

The Russian lumbered down an iron stairway that
ran along the hull at an angle, ending at a small float
about halfway down the length of the ship. I cut the
engine and drifted up to bump against the float. The
Russian came over - he was huge, not just big, with
broad shoulders and a big belly - and stood there grinning. He had on a wool P-coat and a furry Russian hat.

"Toss him the line, Ricky."

Ricky fished the rope out of the bow and flipped it
to the Russian, who knelt down gingerly and tied us off.
Then he struggled up again and waved us onto the float.
"Hello!" he boomed. "Come and visit!"

I made a maitre-de's gesture toward the float.
"After you."

"I'm gonna wait here," Ricky said.

I gave him a look but he just squeezed his eyes
shut and crossed his arms. He'd remembered he was
angry with me and he was annoyed that he'd let himself
have a good time on the river.

I climbed out, walked over to where the Russian
sat cross-legged on the float, arranging metal pins,
stamps in little cases, coins and a Red Army wristwatch
on the planks. There were postcards. I picked one up
and could only make out one word – Murmansk - on its
back. There were Perestroika medals with tiny
Gorbachev heads. Then there was this razor. I picked it
up and twisted the stem, and the blade-holder yawned
open. I liked the razor. I'd been using disposables in the

apartment over the pool hall.

"We trade?" the Russian said. "Good capitalists, da?"

"Maybe." I looked over my shoulder. Ricky was talking to himself with his chin in his hands, making his whole head move. He looked a little nutty, sitting there with his head bouncing around.

"Something for boy! Is nice boy, yes?"

"He's mad at me right now."

The Russian winked, pushed himself to his feet and clumped over to the boat. Ricky gawked up. The Russian held his hand out. "Come and give to Victor all of your money!" He laughed and wriggled his fingers.

Ricky took his hand and stepped onto the float.

This Victor bent way down and grabbed his shoulder. "What is matter?"

Ricky shrugged under the weight of his paw.

Victor patted him lightly. "Everything?"

Ricky's mouth twisted a little.

"Whole bloody world?" Victor said. "Yes?"

Ricky smiled.

"So." Victor marched Ricky toward me. Picking up the watch, he said, "Look, is nice Russian watch." He slapped it into Ricky's hand.

"It's got the CCCP!"

"CCCP." Victor shook his head. "Is big breakup. Is many problems." He ruffled Ricky's hair, squinted at me.

"Your son?"

"My son in Murmansk." Victor told us that it seemed Dmitri was a foot taller every time Victor went home. His son, he said, would be a man before he got to go back this time.

"My Dad's away, too," Ricky piped up.

Victor raised bushy eyebrows.

"Separated," I admitted. "Listen, how much for the watch?"

Victor leaned close. "Was belonging to crew from Estonia. Was in Army. But hates Army." He scowled. "Better for boy. So, special deal. Only fifty dollars!"

"Fifty bucks?"

Now Ricky was staring at me.

"All right," I said.

Victor straightened up. "Good! Victor is rich now!"

Ricky grinned.

"Something else?" Victor growled.

I hunkered down to look. The float rocked a little in the cool breeze. It was chillier out here on the salt water. Victor rubbed his hands together and blew into them.

"Choose! Nice pins. Rubles. Medals."

I picked up the razor. It had a broad handle that felt good in my hand. I kind of liked the idea of shaving with a razor made in a far-away country.

Victor shut one eye. "Is ten."

I leaned sideways and pulled out my wallet. I'd had a good night shooting nine-ball with a couple of kids from the shoeshop, and there were three twenties, along with a few ones and a ten.

Victor looked at my money.

I gave him the twenties. "We'd better get going."

Ricky was raising and lowering his arm, letting the watch slide up and down. Then he pushed it onto the base of his hand. "Thanks, Victor!" he said.

Victor held out his arms and Ricky jumped right over and hugged him. I was a little jealous. Ricky hadn't hugged me like that since I'd left home. Victor held him tight, then turned him loose and ducked his head. He took a swipe at his eyes with the sleeve of his P-coat.

We headed for the boat, with Victor close behind, looking somber. Ricky stepped aboard and Victor grabbed my arm before I could follow. I was a little scared, he was such a big bastard. But he only wanted to tell me something. He nodded toward the center of the float and tugged me away from the boat. He cleared his throat, looked at Ricky, then back at me. He leaned down close and said, "Listen, I know it's none of my business."

"What happened to your voice?" I said.

The peasant accent was gone. He sounded more British than anything now. I took a quick look at Ricky, but he was busy working the buttons on his new watch.

"Never mind my voice. You and your boy. I don't know your circumstances, of course. But I gather you've split up the family in some way or other."

"We had a little trouble," I said.

"Don't we all? But listen, I don't want to offend, but make sure you think things over carefully. It's so easy to do the wrong thing. You seem like a nice chap and one who loves his son, and your son reminds me so much of mine or I wouldn't bother."

"Okay," I said.

"You might have your nose out of joint," Victor said. "Or she might. Maybe you're enjoying your freedom right now. But you'll be surprised at how fast it goes. You won't believe how fast."

I was still having trouble with his voice. With his heavy eyebrows and potato nose he still looked like a peasant. But he sounded educated. "Well, thanks for the advice," I said. "I appreciate it."

"Don't patronize me." His grip on my arm tightened.

"I'm not. I believe you. It's going to go fast."

"Especially once he gets used to it. You'll be off doing your own thing, and all the while he'll be growing up and before long you'll be this sort of uncle who drops in occasionally. Then you'll realize it's gone too far and then, when you've lost your chance, that's when it will break your bloody heart."

"Is that what happened to you?"

"Yes!" he said. "Why do you think I'm telling you all this?"

"All right." I looked down at my arm, which he still gripped.

He held me within whispering range for a moment longer, then sighed and let go. We walked back to the boat. I shook his hand, got in and he untied us and tossed the line aboard. Then he put a boot on the rail and shoved us off. "Goodbye!" he said to Ricky in his peasant voice.

"Bye!" Ricky said. "Thanks for the watch!"

"Is okay!" Victor waved, then lost the goofy grin and pointed seriously at me. I nodded. Then I twisted around to yank the starter cord. The motor gurgled and water swelled and bubbled off the stern and we headed off. Ricky kept waving until we'd rounded the high, sharp prow.

"He was nice," Ricky said.

"Come show me that watch."

He moved back and sat beside me. I chanced putting an arm around him as I ducked my head to look. It seemed to be all right. I aimed us in toward the town, holding on lightly so he wouldn't become too aware of it and move away.

The boat ride did the trick, or maybe it was Victor and the watch. Whatever, Ricky loosened up for the rest of the weekend, and by the time I took him back on Sunday he'd been his old cheerful, talkative self for a whole day. I couldn't stand the peace and quiet after he'd gone. I missed him and I missed Suzy, too, but it still hurt like hell when I thought about how I'd caught her. I wished I hadn't caught her. No I didn't. Maybe if it hadn't been her old boyfriend. Old boyfriends know every curve and crease and you can imagine what they want because you've wanted it too. That makes it worse, I think.

That night I stayed up much too late, drinking vodka out of a coffee cup and reading through the book Ricky had left behind. I had the idea if I read what he was reading, I'd feel closer to him.

Next morning I woke up on the couch with a hangover. And I was stiff and sore: it'd been a long time since I'd slept on a couch. When I sat up the empty vodka bottle clonked onto the floor, and when I stood, Ricky's book followed. I picked them both up and shuffled into the bathroom for a quick shower, then made the mistake of trying to shave with my brand-new

Russian razor and cut a gash the size of the Black Sea out of my upper lip. It wouldn't stop bleeding, and finally I gave up, stuck a piece of toilet paper over it and headed off to work.

I couldn't get anything done in the office and finally I shut the door and pulled out Ricky's book again. The next thing I knew it was ten o'clock. I put the book down and walked through the shop, past the pieceworkers.

"Hey Ned, stand too close to the razor this morning?" one yelled above the noise of his machine, and for a moment I didn't know what he was talking about, but then I remembered the shaving cut. I laughed and nodded. He grinned back and never stopped working.

In the men's room I looked in the mirror at the piece of paper stuck to my lip. It had dried a solid red, and as I stared it suddenly began to look exactly like a miniature maple leaf, changed color for fall.

A very curious feeling came over me.

Something rolled over in my mind and the leaf became scale. I suppose my hangover and lack of sleep had something to do with it. Anyway, this huge face stared back at me. Suddenly I saw myself crashing through woods, trailing ropes, tiny leaves flying like confetti around me. This strange notion lasted until somebody else came into the room, and then I lost the idea, it was just a piece of paper stuck to my lip again. I tugged it away from the cut and waited. Nothing happened. But I was afraid if I moved my mouth around, the spot of red would reappear and begin to grow. So I kept the proverbial stiff upper the rest of the day.

It went slowly. It was warm in the shop and there

was nothing to keep my mind off Ricky and Suzy.
When the whistle finally blew, I didn't want to go back
to the empty apartment so I drove through town - past
my house with Suzy's Geo in the driveway - all the way
down to the coast and the little town on the bay where
we'd met Victor. I parked at the public landing.

Ah, shoot, I missed my little boy.

The Russian ship was still there, only farther out in
the bay.

I sat on the hood of my car and looked out at it.
There were a couple of little boats nearby, and I wondered if Victor was working some other poor tourist for
cash. I couldn't see the float or the stairway. Maybe he
wasn't working. Maybe he was lying in his bunk,
drinking vodka, thinking about his son. I remembered
his concern and advice, and then I thought about Ricky
and how he'd come around on Sunday, as if he might be
getting used to the new arrangement. As if he might
have given up trying to get me back. I saw the truth of
Victor's words, and a big lump rose in my throat. Then
for a long moment I couldn't breathe; it was as if someone had thrown ropes around my chest.

That night I put Ricky's book in my pocket and set
off walking. I didn't drive because I needed time in case
I was going to back out. It was only three miles or so,
anyway. I hiked down to the light and followed Main
Street out of town. The homes were close together and
then farther apart and set back from the road. Then
there were farms with cow barns and silos. Dogs barked
at me.

Pretty soon I was there.

The house was dark except for a pale yellow light in the kitchen. I couldn't bring myself to go to the door. I'd thought I would knock and say, "Ricky forgot his book." But I knew she would see right through me, and I didn't know if I wanted that to happen.

It was cool, and after a while I had to jump up and down and wave my arms to keep warm. Then my nose started to run. I didn't have any tissues and had to blow it on a rough piece of newspaper that I found in the weeds.

The outside light came on.

Then the door opened and she was standing there holding her robe shut. Her hair was up in the bun she always wore to bed unless she was planning on something. She looked at me for a few seconds. Then she opened her mouth and her words floated down the driveway and across the road. "I know it isn't a salesman this time of night."

I fished the book out of my pocket.

"He's been looking for that," she said.

I walked down the driveway and handed it to her.

"Won't you come in?" she said.

"Are you alone?"

She just looked at me, and I felt small for saying it. In the kitchen the little light in the stove hood was on. I sat at the table while she boiled water for tea. I looked at her in her fuzzy robe, at her square shoulders and the back of her neck.

"I'm so sorry," she said.

I couldn't say anything.

When the kettle whistled she shut the burner off, poured the water and brought a mug of tea for each of

us to the table. Her eyes were shiny. She looked closely
at me then and said, "Your lip is bleeding."

I touched it with a finger.

She dampened a paper towel and dabbed at the cut.
It seemed to stop pretty easily. She sat back down and
waited.

"I cut myself shaving," I said.

She nodded. "What about tonight?"

I bumped my knees on the underside of the table.
"I don't know."

She reached for my hand. "I'm so sorry, Ned. I
wouldn't have done anything really wrong. I know
what I did was wrong enough, but you have to believe
me. I was really just waiting for him to stop and then I
was going to tell him to leave. He had this story and he
got me to let him in, he tricked me because he knew
how to do it, but I was just waiting for him to stop, I
swear."

"I'm not ready to talk about it just yet."

"All right," she said.

"It's not just us, anyway," I said. "It's Ricky."

"Yes." She nodded. "Are you going to stay?"

"I'll sleep on the couch."

"Okay," she said.

It felt strange to be moving through the house in
the dark, knowing all the angles, needing no light. In
the bathroom I groped for a toothbrush, loaded it by
touch and started brushing. Then I remembered the
shaving cut. I didn't want to bleed all over the couch. I
pulled the door softly shut, flipped the wall-switch and
squinted at the mirror. It seemed to be all right. I rinsed

my mouth and headed back to the living room. Suzy had left a blanket and pillows on the couch, and I lay down, imagined Ricky finding me there in the morning.

I drew up my knees, shut my eyes. It was so still. Back at the apartment I'd still be listening to billiard balls. I drew the blanket to my chin and listened to the quiet house. My eyelids got heavy and I felt sleep coming on, and I snored once and woke myself but then faded quickly back to sleep.

Sometime when it was still dark I woke up again. I'd been dreaming and I lay there trying to remember, and then it came back to me that I'd dreamed I was a giant, on an island.

There were little red leaves all around.

Something was going on out on the water, and I easily broke free of my ropes and hiked down to the shore. It was night in my dream. I could feel cool sand on my feet. I looked out to sea and saw the Russian ship, all lit up, canted over, in trouble on a reef.

I waded right out after it.

The water was cold, and it rose to my chest, but no higher and I kept going, pushing with my thighs, swinging my arms wide. As I drew near I moved carefully, so as not to swamp it with my man-made waves. I bent down carefully to look in the ship's tiny windows. Then I cradled the vessel gently in my enormous hands.

Jon-Clod

We trooped into the house to find my mother in front of the stove with her arms crossed and my father leaning against the sink, hands stuffed deep into his pockets, pipe jutting at an acute angle from his mouth. Neither spoke or looked at us, and we kept moving, filing into the living room and settling ourselves around the TV to watch the Winter Olympics. It was what we had planned to do anyway, why we had hurried back from Old Lady Twing's farm. We loved the pageantry of the Olympics and we loved all the athletes, from the gliding skaters and the plunging, breakneck skiers to the biathletes: cold-eyed masters of that strange, hybrid event. Normally, with the Olympics on TV, nothing less than a house-fire could have diverted our attention, and on this day the TV hadn't been on for five minutes before my siblings had forgotten all about the thickened atmosphere we had come upon in the kitchen. But I was twelve that winter.

It was different for me.

I leaned out over the arm of the couch and cocked an ear toward the doorway. And when I heard my father say, "I thought we were all done with that," the bitter tone of his words, ricocheting down the short hall, was an immediate reward for my effort.

I listened harder.

"Well, so did I," my mother said.

"I've got two jobs now," my father said.

This was too intriguing.

I abandoned the Olympic coverage, slipped through the doorway into the hall and stood near the stairway - so that I could veer left and up the stairs if noticed, as if I were just heading to the bathroom - and I peered into the kitchen, curious as to what they looked like, arguing.

Their faces were as drawn and tight as those of the biathletes, balancing on their skis, squinting along the stocks of their rifles.

"You and your..." My father bit down on his pipe to keep from saying something. But it was too late: my mother threw her wooden spoon to the floor and fled the room. I heard her slam the shed door and I waited, holding my breath, to see what my father would do.

He took the pipe out of his mouth and swore.

I squared my shoulders and walked into the kitchen.

My father was still leaning against the sink. As I walked past him he crossed his arms and puffed a cloud of smoke from his mouth and looked sideways at me.

"Should Mom be outside without her coat?" I

asked casually.

"If she wants to," my father said.

I swallowed hard, but didn't run.

My father sat down at the kitchen table, tapped his fingers on the formica. Then, after a moment, he pushed himself up and went to the window that faced the front lawn. I followed him and we looked out at the trail of blue-ish footprints that led from the road over our lawn past the big pine to the shed. Those were the tracks we kids had left. Then there was another, single trail going around the corner of the shed.

"Did you and Mom have a fight?"

His big eyebrows arched over the rims of his glasses. "I guess we did."

"What about?"

"I don't think I want to say."

He wandered back to the table, drummed his fingers. Then he grunted and returned to the window. I stayed at his side, full of myself. Even the Olympics couldn't compare to this. We looked out together at the yard, but she still wasn't in sight. Then there was a racket from the living room, somebody bickering, and when my father only sighed I went in and shouted them to silence.

Back in the kitchen my father gave me a flat look.

"Damn brats," I said.

The fighting started up again. My father shook his head. I went back into the living room. "Dad and I have had about enough," I said. They looked at me as if I were a stranger, and one they might possibly have to obey. Only my brother Jimmy dared to sneer.

"So wise-up, people." I went back to my father.

"They'll be good now," I said.

"Sure they will."

His tone bothered me. "What are you, mad at us too?" I said.

He didn't deny it, sat there silently, and I, testing my new status, allowed myself to get angry with him. I put my hands on my hips and said, "Well, that's just great."

"Don't push your luck," my father said.

I stared back at him, but when he didn't look away or modify his weary expression all my courage left. I let tears show in my eyes and then ran into the hall and up the stairs to the room I shared with two of my brothers. I threw myself down on my bed, waiting to hear him climb the stairs to apologize. But instead I heard the front door shut very hard, and then the car starting. Then it got quiet and I could hear the TV from the room below. They had it turned up loud and I could hear the announcer talking excitedly about the skiers.

Jean-Claude Killy was the main reason Jimmy and I got up early every Saturday and walked the half-mile to Twing's Farm and out the pasture to the twin hills flanking Spar Creek (the other kids tagging along unimportantly, dilettantes with their saucers and sleds.) We were French on our mother's side and he was a hero to her and had become one to us, too. I tried to ski like Killy, walk like Killy; I gave myself pep talks with a French accent. I even practiced smiling like Killy, trying desperately to force a long dimple into my cheek. But this effort made me look more like a chipmunk than a world-class skier. Even worse, my brother Jimmy

caught me standing in front of the mirror, contorting my
grin, and knowing immediately - probably he harbored
similar fantasies - what I was up to, he began calling me
Jon-Clod, his tone leaving no doubt as to the spelling he
had in mind. This nickname, unfortunately, was so apt
that everyone in the family - even my father, whom I
would never have suspected capable of such treachery -
began to use it.

Anyway, warmed by our half-mile walk, we would
reach the farm and cross the pasture to the hills where
the creek trickled into Casco Bay, and we would don
our old, inherited wooden skis and set off at an angle
down the hill, traversing the slope to make the run
longer, finally crossing the frozen surface of the creek
at the bottom. Then we would walk up opposite sides of
the miniature valley, our skis on our shoulders; and then
we would ski down again. We had to keep a straight
path on our descent, because the old leather bindings
would twist if we tried to turn, and then we would fall.

After ski-ing hard all morning, we would brush
ourselves off, gather our equipment - or most of it,
something usually got left behind - and tramp home,
ready for the hot soup and sandwiches our mother
prepared on such outdoor days.

As we walked, passing cars would honk. We were
an old Pequot family and everybody knew us, and they
were amused by this long procession of Williams
children tramping along the wintery road, skis on
shoulders, towing sleds and saucers. We wouldn't
respond because we were a little ashamed that there
were so many of us. It had become a bit of a town joke.
In Church it was always embarrassing the way they

watched us come down the aisle. I remember my mother walking very straight at the head of her brood, and then waiting by the end of the row as we filed past to our seats. We filled an entire pew, even without my father, who was agnostic and wouldn't go.

Not long after my father drove off, my mother returned from wherever she'd gone and made the usual sandwiches and ladled out the soup and we kids - my unseen tears had dried quickly and I'd returned to the living room to finish watching the Killy win the Giant Slalom - trooped into the kitchen and ate. Our mother was quiet but civil enough that I decided definitely to take her side of the dispute, whatever it had been about. Once that decision had been made I didn't dwell on it.

After we finished eating we headed back to the farm and resumed our work toward some future Olympics. The Giant Slalom had freshened our determination, and we made faster runs than ever before down the hills. We even staged medal ceremonies after particularly brilliant performances, standing on creek rocks near the mouth of the stream, bending our heads toward an imaginary official, holding ourselves in dignified bows while the ribbons were placed around our necks, straightening to look firmly but kindly out over the applauding spectators, poor souls who would never know such glory.

Of course we had to take turns standing on the highest rock, there could be only one winner, and this inevitably became cause for conflict, over whose turn it happened to be, and soon we were rolling around on the ski-packed snow, slapping and kicking and conniving for the headlock that would end the matter.

We fought for fifteen or twenty minutes.

The little kids ignored us and kept sliding, but several of Old Lady Twing's cows, recently released from the barn, gathered at the nearest electric fence to watch.

Finally I maneuvered an arm under Jimmy's chin, grabbed my fist with the other hand and squeezed until he had to give in or black out. Then I let him go. When the sun went down behind the trees we headed back.

In the kitchen my parents were hugging, although not equivalently: my mother's eyes were closed and her face pressed hard against my father's chest; he, on the other hand, held her gingerly and there was still a touch of melancholy in his eyes. But it appeared the disagreement had come to some kind of closure.

They separated when we banged into the house, asked us how the sliding had been - I was very offended by this inadequate description - and smiled tiredly at their mob of children moving through the kitchen and into the living room, oblivious - all but me - to the rending and mending of the fabric of their marriage that day. I stayed behind to see what came next, pretending to look through the pile of mail next to the telephone on the counter.

My father glanced at my mother, who nodded; then he came over and put a hand on my shoulder. "I'm sorry about before," he said, looking down at me, his eyes big behind the lenses of his glasses. "It's just that I got taken by surprise."

I remembered then that I was mad at him, that he

had not only argued with my mother and practically admitted that he hated us all, but had committed the even worse sin of neglecting to come to my room and comfort me. But I couldn't stay angry with him so close and touching me; indeed, I felt a sob quivering around inside, for some reason, and had to nod and blink in response.

"Tell him what surprised you, John," my mother said.

I stared at the linoleum.

"Johnny," my father said, "you're going to be a brother again."

He laughed softly, squeezed my shoulder.

I found this news bewildering. Jo-Jo, our youngest, was four now and I could barely remember his coming home from the hospital and it had never occurred to me, despite all the living proof, that it might happen again. I managed to square myself away long enough to look at my father. "What do you want with another kid?"

He laughed again. "Ask your mother." He reached to touch the back of her neck, then ruffled my hair, then walked past me to the shed. I saw him grab his wool coat off the wall and go outside.

I looked at my mother.

"A child," she said, "is a gift from God."

"Oh," I said.

"Tomorrow in Church we'll give thanks." She gestured toward a vase of flowers, some arrangement my father had evidently brought home as a peace offering. "See what I got?"

"Uh-huh," I said.

She primped them, pulled a long-stemmed, blue

one out and stuck it back in a different place.

"How come Dad never comes to Church?" I said.

"Dad's not Catholic like us."

"Oh yeah," I said.

My mother went into the living room and turned off the TV long enough to tell the rest of the kids about the baby. Jimmy rolled his eyes at me. The younger ones started planning whose room to keep it in. My mother turned the TV back on and went upstairs.

I headed outside.

My father wasn't sitting on the shed steps smoking, which had been my assumption. I looked around the yard, and he wasn't leaning against the oak with the birdfeeder, nor the big pine by the crossing; he wasn't sitting in the slatted lawn chair next to the clothesline; he wasn't in any of his habitual quiet places.

So he must, I thought, be taking a walk.

I zipped my jacket, pulled my hood up, started across the crusty lawn. There was a breeze rattling the bare branches of the oak. I walked out onto the blacktop and looked back at the tree, stark against the yellow-lit windows of our house. Then I set off down the road, knowing which way he'd go, it had to be toward South Pequot, he never walked the other way because the highway was less than a half-mile in that direction and he hated the highway.

The moon was up, nearly full, bright in the sky.

I walked along, the cold air on my face, looking left and right for signs of my father. But he wasn't anywhere. I walked all the way down to Old Lady Twing's without seeing or hearing him, and began to wonder if he had, on this unique day, decided to change his habit and roam down to the highway and watch - as I did from my bedroom window sometimes - the stream of headlights heading north. But then I heard something, a scraping, icy noise, which after a moment I recognized.

I jumped the cow fence and started across the pasture toward the creek, walking on a sheen of moonglow, the snowcrust solid under my feet. The sounds came again, louder, then stopped and I heard him crunching back up the hill, heard him breathing, heard the lightened scratch of the sled behind him. It would have to be the new Flyer, the brats must have left it behind, that would be the only one big enough for him, and I could picture him towing it up the hill by its long rein.

I laughed to myself, hurried along.

I reached the shallow ravine where the creek ran through the pasture, and followed it, having in mind to run out and surprise him, to join him for a ride or two. How poignant, to go sliding with your father at night. What a great coup, how wonderful it would be to tell Jimmy in the morning, how jealous and spiteful it would make him. I could picture my father smiling as I ran out into the open. "Well, look who's here!" he might say. "How about a ride?"

The thought quickened my pulse, my step. But when I got to the deepened, broadened mouth of the creek and saw him poised on the hill, holding the sled, caught in the moonlight, ready to go, I changed my mind. He seemed so boyish in his posture, so content in his aloneness that I knew if I ran out laughing, interrupting his nostalgic, childish sledding, he wouldn't smile and greet me, ask me to join him on the sled, speed down the hill with his arms around me. No, he wanted to be alone. He'd be nice enough. But he'd probably say, "What are you doing out this late, Jon-Clod?"

And he'd stop what he was doing and then he'd go home.

I couldn't bear the thought of that. So I sat down on the snow to watch, my back against a fencepost. And then, after he'd flung himself downhill, the sled blades very loud and cutting in the still night, and after he'd made his heavy, accelerating run to the bottom and halfway up the other side, and especially after the whoop he'd let out as he crossed the creek at his top speed; after all this I could no more have shown myself than - had I been one of those Norwegians, those tight-faced, foreign biathletes - I could have unstrapped my rifle from my shoulder, taken aim as he climbed to the top of the far side of the hill, and shot him.

Orion

Frank mimicked a woman's shrill, naggy voice: "'It ain't nothing but an excuse to drink beer.' That's what she says every time." He was explaining the argument that had made him late for ice fishing. He'd rehearsed his explanation, walking out from the road, following the Rebel's footprints onto the ice and up to the shack in the middle of the small lake, showing up an hour later than he'd promised.

"Speaking of beer." The Rebel tossed an empty out the door of the shack. He dug his heels in the ice, squirmed on the up-ended orange crate, held out a hand.

Frank tore one free of the plastic rings, passed it over.

The Rebel popped it open, guzzled half. He wiped his mouth with the back of his hand, reached to turn up the little kerosene heater. The sun was low, and it was getting chilly in the shack on the ice.

"Christ," he said, "I was some thirsty."

"I never should've gotten married again." Frank looked down at his boots, then gazed out the door of the shack at the tip-ups. He and the Rebel had set ten of them, working fast after Frank's belated arrival, cutting foot-wide holes to the lakewater with his smoky, gas-powered ice auger. Now, as the sun was setting, the flags were hard to see, even against the white snow over the ice. Behind the lake the sun illuminated the crown of Ragged Mountain.

The Rebel nodded. "No reason for anyone to be a three-time loser."

Frank looked at him. "How'd you know about that?"

The Rebel shrugged. Probably he'd heard it from one of the other cabbies. Between flights, sitting around on the old baggage belt, playing hearts, there was a lot of gossip, usually about whoever was off on a trip.

Frank said, "You ever been married?"

The Rebel laughed silently, shaking his head.

"You didn't leave some girl back home?"

"Not me."

"How old are you?" Frank asked. The shack was only the size of a two-hole outhouse, and it was easy to ask questions when you'd been sitting there together in the cold, drinking beer, watching for the tip-ups to show.

So far they'd caught nothing.

"Twenty-eight," the little guy said. "Why, you going to ask me out?"

"You're not my type," Frank said.

"Oh, Jethuth," the Rebel lisped. "I'm crushed."

Frank shook his head. He was used to the Rebel's humor now. At first some of the cabbies had resented him, the way he'd started driving with no apparent shyness or modesty, but that hadn't lasted long. He was a funny guy. Everyone soon got to like him.

"How come you never got married?" Frank took his watchcap off, brushed his hair behind his ears, put the cap back on. He'd worn his hair long since the late Sixties. In college several girls had told him it was too pretty for a guy, that it was wasted on him, and he'd been quietly proud of it ever since.

"Because I'm a goddamn fairy." The Rebel suddenly reached over and laid a limp hand on Frank's leg.

Frank jerked his leg away.

The Rebel chortled and drank some beer. He stood up and drop-kicked the empty out the door of the shack onto the frozen lake. Quite a collection was forming out there. "Three points," the Rebel said, mincing back inside. "Ain't you impressed, dear?"

"Sometimes I wonder," Frank said.

The Rebel stumbled over to Frank and sat on his lap.

Frank stood up and watched in horror as the Rebel slid down his legs to the ice. "For Chrissake, Rebel!"

"You're cute when you're angry," the Rebel said from the floor.

Frank stomped out the door. He went around to all of the tip-ups, checking their tripping mechanisms, taking a long time. None had been triggered. He looked back at the shack and could see the slight red glow of the heater. The sky was dark now and the first stars were showing. He couldn't see Orion yet, though. Orion was the only constellation he knew, except for the Big and Little Dippers - which didn't count because anybody could find them - and because of that he always took a quiet pleasure in finding it in the night sky. He thought of it as his personal constellation. He walked back to the shack, the snowcrust squeaky under his boots. Inside, he sat down on the crate, after moving it a little farther away from the Rebel.

"How about a beer?" the Rebel said.

"Okay."

They popped the cans: two small vacuums were gone.

"You ought not to fool around so much," Frank said. "Can't you ever just sit and talk?"

"Sure I can."

"You'd never know it."

The Rebel laughed. "Come on."

"Really. All you ever do is fool around."

"What's wrong with that?"

"Nothing, unless it's all you do."

The Rebel held up his hands. "Hey, if you don't like my company..."

"I like your company," Frank said. "But there's no crime in just talking a little. We don't always have to be telling a joke or whatever." Frank shut his mouth, wondered why he was, all at once, so upset.

The Rebel lit a cigarette, his face yellowing behind the match. He blew the match out, dragged on the cigarette, the red coal glowing in the darkness of the shack.

Frank spoke more evenly: "You see what I mean, don't you? We're friends. We can talk without making a joke of it all the time. There are two intelligent human beings sitting here."

The Rebel said: "Who's the other one?"

Frank threw up his hands. He was still holding a can of beer, and some of it slopped out onto the icy floor of the shack.

The Rebel pointed. "Watch your beer there."

Frank ignored this comment. "You got to take yourself seriously," he said, "or no one else will."

"I don't care if they take me serious."

"Of course you do."

"I do not."

"Everybody wants to be taken seriously."

The Rebel thought for a moment. "Groucho Marx," he said then.

Frank just looked at him. Then he shook his head sadly. He finished his beer and popped another one open. He drank, muttered to himself.

"Well?" the Rebel said.

"He's a goddamn comedian! That doesn't count."

"Oh, so you're changing the rules."

"I'm not changing anything!"

"You said everybody wants..."

"I know what I said!"

"I'm going out and check the holes." The Rebel left the shack, headed out across the snow. Frank turned the heater down. He was plenty warm now. There was a buzz in his ears. He stepped to the doorway and looked up, turning his head until he saw the three diagonal stars and then the rest of the constellation. He smiled to himself: it was nice to have a design like that in the sky, that you could find any time the stars were out.

He sat back down, drank some more beer.

Pretty soon the Rebel came back.

"Anything?"

"Nope." He sat down.

"Want a beer?"

"Sure," the Rebel said. "Too cold to dance." He grinned.

"They're not biting," Frank said. He was trying to get the conversation back on a reasonable plane. There was no sense to argue about something as stupid as comedians.

"Sometimes they don't," the Rebel said.

They sat drinking.

"What time you got?" Frank asked.

When the Rebel looked at his watch he dumped beer in his lap.

Frank burst into laughter.

The Rebel had to laugh, too.

"What a Frenchman!" Frank said, when he could talk.

"Hell, you did the same thing two minutes ago."

"That was an hour ago! And I just slopped a little, I didn't dump a whole can in my lap. Jesus!   Frenchman!"

"So what the hell's your name?" the Rebel said. "Frank LaCombe."

"Well, what about your name?"

"Miller ain't a French name."

"What is it, then?" Frank challenged.

"I don't know," the Rebel said. "English. It ain't French."

"It means Homo in French," Frank said.

They looked at each other, then exploded in laughter. It seemed to be the funniest thing either of them had ever heard. The Rebel fell off the crate, laughing, bumped Frank's crate and Frank spilled onto the cold floor, too. They ended up pounding each other on the back, and when they stood up their arms were entwined. They stood laughing, holding on like two drunks trying to cross a street, weaving on their feet.

"Ohhh, Jesus!" the Rebel gasped.

"My side!"

They grinned at each other, their faces only inches apart. Then the Rebel squeezed Frank tightly and pressed his cheek against Frank's. For an instant, this was all right, it was a joke, they continued to chuckle. But when the Rebel didn't let go within a reasonable time, Frank began to struggle. Then the Rebel released him. They went back to their crates and sat down. The Rebel cleared his throat. Frank held a beer out, and the Rebel took it. They opened their beers and drank. The Rebel turned the heater up. After a little while they began conversing again in small increments.

The Rebel said, "Good beer."

"Yeah."

"I like that Nasty-gansett."

"Nice and cold," Frank said.

They sat drinking, listening to the ice grinding and snapping across the lake. Then the Rebel said, "Wonder if we caught anything?"

"I don't know."

"Not that it really matters."

"That's what my wife says."

"Let's go check the holes." The Rebel looked out

the door.

There were no fish. On the way back Frank looked up in the sky, and for a moment could not find Orion. He spun around, looking. Then he saw it. It had just moved a little. It was still there.

Inside the shack things were pretty much back to normal. They kept at the beer. They cracked jokes and laughed. They got drunker. They talked about Frank's latest wife. They drank all the beer and then the Rebel broke out a pint of Philadelphia whiskey and they started in on that. They told more jokes and laughed. But they were careful not to laugh so hard they'd fall off the crates again. Around midnight they finally caught a strange fish with one eye, and when Frank tried to take it off the hook, it bit him.

Jade

One fall Paul Waterman found that he could tramp the woods again, and that November he was even able to draw a bead on a fat doe cropping grass on the other side of Dodge Ridge. He held the scope dead on the doe's shoulder - in closeup there were worn patches in its dun coat - and for a long moment there was no panic. But then he felt the pressure in his skull, and he saw bony-faced soldiers charging uphill past torn brush and shell-pocked ground. It was blazing hot on the hill, and the same old people began falling around him.

Johnny Lavers spun and dropped. Johnny's jade bracelet - stolen from a gook princess, he'd said - slipped out from under his shirtsleeve, a beautiful green against the dirt. Then Curtis Haines, wonder in his eyes, rolled sideways and released a trickle of crimson onto the dust at the foot of the sandbags. Finally, Fattie Hansen keeled over and, settling, let loose a long, windy flatulence, as if his soul were taking that method of escape.

Paul wrestled the images to a halt.

He lowered the rifle, walked out into the meadow. The deer lifted its head, stepped into the woods and was gone. Paul sat on a pulpy stump at the edge of the field, smoking cigarette after cigarette until he felt capable of hiking home. Then he walked out of the woods to the road and the lake. There were cormorants on the lake, holding their wings out to dry.

In the bedroom Paul's wife put her paperback facedown on the quilt. "I didn't shoot anything," Paul said.

"Good," she said, picking the book up again.

Joyce thought it was silly, all this recent tramping of the woods. But then, she thought the jade bracelet had come from a shop in Tokyo. He'd just never been able to talk about it. Once, six years after coming home, he'd tried a seminar called Healing the Vietnam Veteran at the Community College, but the man there had wanted them to embrace one another, and Paul had hightailed it, deciding he would rather deal with it on his own. And it had gotten better over the years, although the panic still was apt to visit when he did anything resembling a war-time activity, and he still sometimes felt, at the onset of sleep, that his soul might rush out through the top of his head.

But that day, looking through the scope at the deer, something had been different. It hadn't come immediately. He'd almost had to summon it. He thought about that at work and driving home past the ridge, and he began making plans for the next weekend.

On Saturday Paul hiked through the lake and hill country to the ridge, ready to try it again. He hunted the whole morning, working around The Bog and then the meadow and the woods on the back side of the ridge. Then that afternoon, just to be thorough, he checked the east side of the ridge where it was rocky and steep, where you normally wouldn't expect to find a deer anyway. And he didn't.

But he found something else.

It started with a whiff of smoke at twilight. Paul followed the scent across the slope to an outcropping of rusty-colored ledge and a small, flat cave.There was a fire in the cave, its shifting light on the rock wall. Someone was inside, humming the Battle Hymn of the Republic, and Paul held still a few feet away to listen nostalgically. The voice imitated various brass instruments. It was quite a performance, and when it was over, Paul clapped his hands.

It was quiet in the cave.

A cat's paw breeze rattled the shallow covering of leaves on the rock shelf, then swept down and traced a cold, soft pattern across Paul's cheek.

"Everything all right in there?" Paul said finally.

"No," the man inside said. "Everything ain't all right. I'm about to swell up and die. But I thought I'd have some supper first, if that's all right with you."

"You don't have to get sarcastic," Paul said.

The fire snapped loudly.

"What are you doing here, anyway?" Paul said.

"You own this mountain?"

"No," Paul said.

"Then what do you care?"

"I hunt here."

"La-de-da," the man said.

"I smelled your fire," Paul said. "Came over to see who was scaring the deer away."

"Ain't no deer on this ridge."

"How do you know?"

"I know, don't you worry," came the voice from the cave. It had the ironic tone Paul remembered, and for an instant his vision narrowed. But he managed to hold it off by biting his lip.

"I ain't from around here, maybe," the voice went on, "but I know."

"What are you doing in Maine anyway?"

"I can go anywhere I want."

"All right, brother," Paul said.

"Who you calling brother?"

"That guy beside you," Paul said.

The man in the cave laughed. He was silent for a long moment, then said, "When were you In Country?"

"'68, '69."

"Whereabouts?"

"Here and there."

"Tell me some place I know."

"You ever hear of Dong Ha?"

"Don't get sensitive."

"Who's sensitive?" Paul said. "Not me."

"Marines?"

"2nd Battalion, 1st Marines, I Corps," Paul recited.

The fire chuckled. Overhead, branches rattled together. "You better come on in and have a drink," the man in the cave said.

The man introduced himself as Edgar Turgeon,

and he and Paul shook hands, thumbs up. Edgar pulled
a bottle out of his rucksack, poured a trickle into a
metal cup and handed it to Paul.

The whiskey was warm and tasted slightly of tin.

"Where's the smoke go?" Paul said, handing the
cup back.

"There's a crack overhead. It goes up through
there."

Edgar screwed the cap back on the bottle, slapping
it lightly with his fingers, and put it away. "So how you
like my place?" he said, grinning.

Paul looked at the back of the cave. On one side of
a mattress was a dresser with its third drawer missing.
There were paperbacks and a hurricane lamp on the
dresser. A rumpled sleeping bag lay on the mattress.
Tacked to the side of the dresser was a glossy postcard
picturing a long black wall etched with names, and Paul
leaned backward to look at it.

Paul turned back. "How long you been here?"

"Month," Edgar Turgeon said.

"How'd you wind up here?"

"Came to pick apples," Edgar said with a laugh. "I
quit that gig. One of the bums in town told me about
this place: I guess he stayed here before."

Paul looked around again. "Winter's coming."

"I'll be back in Florida," Edgar said. "Picking
oranges."

Paul watched the fire: yellow flames crowned the
embers.

"You know, I was there same time as you," Edgar
said.

Paul felt a tightening of his temples. There was a

hill, smack in the middle of a valley. From the hill they could see troops crossing the DMZ, two divisions, steady and purposeful. He held his hands out to the coals. Beside him Edgar cleared his throat, pawed the rucksack open and took out the bottle again.

"No thanks," Paul said.

"Maybe I'll just have a spot myself." Edgar tipped the bottle up, holding it with two fingers and a thumb. He swallowed, recapped it, stuck it away. "You look like you're doing okay," he said.

"I'm doing okay."

"Do you think about it?"

Paul shook his head. They were frantically scraping the shallow topsoil away, hacking at the rock and clay beneath. They filled sandbags, built them higher. Everyone was swearing: "What the fuck are we doing in this mother-fucking place?"

"Guess you don't live in no cave, either."

"Nope," Paul said.

"Got you a family?"

"Wife."

Edgar looked at the rucksack and frowned. "Man," he said, "I ain't had a shower in I don't know how long."

Paul stared at the red and black coals. Drinking beer in a cave was one thing, taking Edgar home with him quite another. But he considered it, before shaking his head and saying, "Can't do it."

Edgar nodded.

"The wife, you know."

"Sure," Edgar said.

"I better hit the road, in fact." Paul got to his feet and walked bent-over to the entrance. He looked back.

"Could you use a couple bucks?"

Edgar chuckled.

Paul tipped his wallet toward the coals, selected a bill. "I can let you have a fin."

Edgar took it with two fingers. "Much obliged."

"You take it easy."

"Drop by any time," Edgar said.

Paul ducked out of the cave. The stars were out. The little breeze had quit and it was still and cold. Paul moved tree to tree down the ridge, like a man on point. Artillery fell from the high ground on both sides of the hill. He couldn't be moving downhill because of the NVA. But he was moving downhill. Then he stepped out of the woods and it was clear of brush down to the lake and there were cars moving along the road, pushing stubby beams of light.

Two days later Paul hiked back to the cave. It was cold and overcast and he wondered if snow was on the way. Snow made tracking the deer so much easier. But he could smell Edgar's fire again, and knew the deer would be skittish and if he did find one it would have to be in the Bog, where everyone and his cousin hunted.

"Yo, Edgar," he said from the cave entrance.

"Entre vous," Edgar said.

Paul stooped and entered the cave. The fire was burned low. Edgar lay on the mattress reading; he sat up and put the book face down on the dresser. "I was just fixing to eat," he said. "Waiting on the coals. You hungry?"

"Already ate," Paul said. "But I'll have a beer with you."

He'd decided that five dollars was not sufficient.

"Well, all right!" Edgar grasped the handle of an iron frying pan that was out of sight behind the dresser. He scooched to the fire and rested it on the rocks over the coals. There was a mixture in the pan and as it heated Paul could smell hamburger and onions and peppers, and spices he couldn't name.

Edgar shook the pan like a prospector.

Paul slipped his backpack off, pulled out a 16-ounce can and opened it. Edgar took it with his free hand and drank. Paul opened one for himself.

Paul said, "I'm not hungry but it don't smell bad."

"You can have some."

"No, really, I'm not hungry. It just smells good."

Edgar poked at the food with a fork. It had cooked quickly, and he sat back and began eating, picking out the coolest bits first. He said, "Could be C-rats, right?"

"Don't remind me," Paul said.

"Remember ham and lima beans?"

"Ham and motherfuckers," Paul said.

Edgar giggled.

"I couldn't eat nothing but beans and weenies, time I left," Paul said.

Edgar chewed, eyes flicking toward Paul. "Dong Ha was a motherfucker," he said. "You know if it was World War Two, y'all would've been made into a movie or something."

Paul looked at the fire. A coal popped and sparks flew. He was out of ammunition and gathering rocks to throw. The soldiers climbed slowly, using all the cover left in the torn brush and ground, not trusting the apparent exhaustion of the Americans' firepower. They were regular troops with helmets, web gear, uniforms, and Paul swore to see how well-off they looked. Beside him Curtis Haines said, "You do realize we are dead fucking meat." Johnny Lavers looked at Paul, rubbed his good-luck bracelet.

"I bet you thought you were cooked," Edgar said.

Paul scratched his scalp, stared at Edgar. They were in a cave, and there hadn't been any caves, unfor-tunately, on the little hill. He looked out at the leaves on the rock shelf. When it was all gone he smiled at Edgar.

"So," he said in falsetto, "what did you do in the war?"

Edgar laughed.

"Did you ever kill anyone?" Paul said. He was remembering a woman in the IGA who'd cornered him by the produce years ago. She was a reporter for the local weekly, and there was to be a write-up in recogni-tion of the tenth anniversary of Nixon's Peace With Honor.

Edgar laughed, scooped and ate. "I didn't kill nobody," he said. "I was a corpsman."

"You poor bastard," Paul said.

"Hey, my people took good care of me."

"I bet they did."

Edgar, using one tine of the fork, touched the tiny pieces of food left in the pan and lifted them to his mouth.

"I couldn't have done that job," Paul said.

"Man, I still don't know how I did." Edgar put the pan aside. He took another beer from Paul with a nod. He shook his head, laughing at the memory of his foolish job: a corpsman, patching holes and ducking lead.

"I was a radio man for a while," Paul said.

"Yeah?"

"Another walking target."

"Yeah," Edgar said.

Paul could think about this part all right. He could think about the bush and the guys and the sissy lieutenant who made them wait while he puked off to the side of the trail.

Paul threw a crinkly leaf into the coals, watched it flare. "So you were a corpsman, huh?"

Edgar grinned.

Paul sighed. "I suppose you still want that shower?"

"Right on," Edgar said.

In the kitchen Paul yelled, "Joyce, we got company."

After a moment the TV went off and a small, blonde woman looked in at them from the living room.

"This is the guy I told you about," Paul said.

Edgar cleared his throat. "Evenin'," he said.

"Hello," Joyce said cooly. She looked at Paul, then back at Edgar. "It's nice to meet you," she said, and went back into the living room. The TV came back on.

"I told you she wouldn't be wild about it," Paul whispered.

"Maybe I ought to leave."

"Naw, come on." Paul led Edgar down a short hall to the bathroom. The hall seemed cramped with two men in it. Paul opened the door and said, "Go ahead. Use that blue robe when you're done."

Edgar looked in at the robes hanging from pegs in the wall, at the shower curtain covered with swooping gulls."Much obliged," he said.

Paul pulled the door shut, headed for the living room.

Joyce kept her eyes on the TV screen when he came in.

"He was a corpsman," Paul said.

"Whatever that is."

"That," Paul said, "is the guy who crawls out after you when you're hit."

"You weren't hit, that I ever heard."

It struck Paul suddenly, and he went into the kitchen and out onto the deck. He sat down on the bench, squeezed his eyes shut hard. Then it all started over again. His friends began falling around him: Johnny Lavers and Curtis Haines and Fattie Hansen, farting his way to heaven. Distantly, through the deck doorway, he heard Joyce say, "He'll probably use up all the hot water."

"I see you found the shaver," Paul said when Edgar came out of the steamy bathroom in the blue robe. Joyce had been right about the hot water; he'd tested it in the kitchen sink. And now here was Edgar, his cheeks plump without their stubble. Paul looked past him at the shaver, back in its holder on the sink.

"I didn't want to get all cleaned up and then not shave."

"Uh-huh."

"Hope you don't mind."

"It's all right.There's clothes in the bedroom," Paul

said, and rattled the green trash bag he'd brought. "I'll put your old stuff in here."

"I'll do that," Edgar offered.

"I've done worse." Paul waited until Edgar shut the bedroom door, then shook the bag open, spread it with his heels and pushed the pile of greasy clothing between his legs into the bag. He snatched the opening shut, spun the bag and fixed the plastic cinch, all without drawing another breath. Then he carried the bag through the kitchen and threw it out on the deck.

Edgar came out of the bedroom wearing tan slacks, a blue striped shirt and a white v-neck sweater. The pants were just long enough to hide his dirty high-tops. He stood there with his hands in his pockets.

"Not bad," Paul said.

Edgar looked down at himself.

They went into the living room where Joyce sat reading.

"Edgar's going to spend the night," Paul announced.

Edgar and Joyce looked at each other.

"No," Edgar said. "I can't."

"Sure you can," Paul told him.

"You've done too much already."

"I've been thinking it over," Paul said.

Edgar looked at Joyce again.

"He doesn't want to stay, for God's sake," Joyce said.

"I'd feel better if I went back," Edgar said. "Honest."

Paul looked from one to the other.

It was still dark the next morning when Joyce,

returning from the bathroom, stopped suddenly beside the bureau, switched the lamp on and began pawing through her jewelry box. She cried out, waking Paul, who popped up in a sweat and looked around the room, blinking.

"He stole my jade bracelet!" Joyce said.

Paul rolled out of bed and stood rubbing his eyes.

"I told you about bringing him in here!"

Paul grabbed his clothes off the floor, began pulling them on. Joyce threw herself onto the bed. Paul took his rifle from behind the door and went to the hall closet for his jacket and boots. Outside, still not fully awake, he crossed the lawn. It was still night and the air cold on his face. It had snowed lightly over night and he left shallow footprints as he set off.

When Paul reached the foot of the ridge it was just dawn, and he was fully awake from the two-mile hike in the cold air. He was also a bit spooked: a half mile back he'd realized that he was going into the woods, during the season, wearing a brown jacket.

But turning back was not an option.

Paul started up, moving slowly, using trees and scattered boulders for cover. At least the leaves, sodden from the snow, weren't noisy. He reached the spot where he'd first smelled Edgar's campfire. There was no smell of smoke this morning: he'd either left or was still curled up in the sleeping bag. There were no footprints in front of the cave. Paul looked at the rifle in his hand. He couldn't believe the son of a bitch had stolen from him.

All that corpsman bullshit, too, Paul thought.

He looked up the last, short stretch of slope to the cave. It was daylight, now, although the sun still not showing over the hills on the other side of the lake. Sweating from his fast hike, he peered toward the top of the ridge. There were dead trees black against the sky. He checked the slope left and right of him, then ran across the open space, stopping behind a bare-limbed tree. After a moment he ducked his head and went through the low opening.

It was empty. Paul checked the back, behind the dresser, to be sure. The mattress and dresser were still there but the sleeping bag and Edgar's paperback books were gone. Paul hunched toward the fireplace and stuck his hand in the ashes: they were cold and damp. He wiped his fingers on his pantleg, sat down and looked out the cave at the blood-red rim of sun just showing over the hill across the lake. He kicked a leg over the edge and lowered himself out. Then he started back down the hill, carrying his rifle in one hand.

A sudden searing crack from above sent him diving and rolling, sliding through the soggy leaves to a jeep-sized boulder halfway down the slope. He lay holding his breath, looking cross-eyed at the leaves. He was pointed downhill, the blood pounding in his head. Then it started to come on and he closed his eyes. The soldiers charged up the hill, and his friends began to fall. They were all down and he was throwing rocks at the NVA. Then they were breaking through. He saw himself fall down and wrestle Johnny and Curtis and Fattie around him. They were loose and heavy and still sweaty. He lay against the toppled sandbags with his dead, damp friends covering him, feeling them jump as the enemy sprayed their fire around. Then somehow Johnny Lavers's hand was in Paul's face, the bracelet hanging free, and Paul found he had to have it. He worked his hand up and yanked it loose. He clutched it tight and didn't move again until the helicopters came.

When Paul's head cleared he was in Edgar Turgeon's arms.

Edgar let Paul down and stood, wiping his hands on his pants. Paul sat up. His shirt was plastered to his back. He remembered his friends, the hot sweaty wait for the choppers. He remembered taking Lavers's bracelet.

"I thought somebody shot you," Edgar said.

Paul cleared his throat. "Where were you?"

"Up above the cave."

"Watching me."

"Heard the shot, saw you take a tumble."

Paul looked upwards, saw a clump of brush where Edgar must have been hiding. He looked back at Edgar and laughed a little. "You're too well trained," he said.

"Tell me about it."

"You could have been long gone."

"I suppose you think that's funny."

"No," Paul said. "Not a bit."

"Good."

Paul put a hand on the boulder and pushed himself up. There were leaves stuck to his pants and he brushed them off. Meanwhile Edgar fished the bracelet out of his pocket, jostled it clicking and rattling in his hand. When Paul looked at him, he said, "I guess you came after this," and tossed it over.

"Why'd you rip me off?"

"I was just poking around," Edgar said, "and I knew where that came from."

"So?"

"So nothing."

Paul looked at the bracelet, said, "Fuck it," and lobbed it back. Edgar pulled his hands out of his pockets and caught it.He looked at Paul.

"Because you really were a corpsman," Paul said.

Edgar jammed the bracelet into his pocket.

"There were some good men over there," Paul said.

"Damn straight."

A second shot rang out from beyond the ridge top. Paul ducked around behind the boulder. Edgar joined him, and they peered over the rock at the top of the ridge. They waited, but there were no more shots.

"You damn Mainers are crazy," Edgar said.

Paul darted out from behind the boulder, hustled up the hill, found his rifle, brought it back and brushed it off.

Edgar slung the rucksack over his shoulder.

"You want to come back with me?" Paul said.

"And face that woman? I think I'll just head her south."

Paul looked down the hill. Beyond the road a corner of the lake was visible, deep blue, tucked into the woods. There was a hawk gliding high above the lake and the hills.

"Ready?"

"No time like the present."

"Let's move it," Edgar said.

Paul followed him down the slope toward the road. It was easy walking downhill and they moved slowly, from tree to tree, careful but nonchalant, like bored grunts on patrol.

The Rain Barrel

In the spring I always made my way down the stairway to the cellar of my father's empty house, and turned on the bulb above the workbench where his tools hung on the pegboard. The tools were dusty. It was very dim in the cellar even during the daytime, because there were no windows in the rock foundation of the old place, and I was as blind as my old man until the bulb blinked on.

On a small pallet at the end of the workbench lay his outboard, and I would lug it outside to the rain barrel beside the shed and crank it up. It was a special request he'd made his first spring in the nursing home, after he had his second stroke, the one that took his sight and speech. He had written the request in his new handwriting, that was all shaky and slanted, and which was half-and-half, now, English and French. Start up the le moteur, he wrote. Has to be commencez every spring or she won't be no good.

Anyway, I did it every year, because he'd always loved his boat and motor so much, and was thinking of them even now. I wrestled it out through the cellar doors across the lawn to the barrel, cleaned the plugs, filled it with fuel, and pulled the cord until it started. I adjusted the mix and left it running for a while; got it going no matter what the weather, so I could tell Papa everything was okay. For four years I did that.

The last year it started raining while I was driving over. It had been raining for a week, then stopped and looked as though it would clear, so I headed off. It was Saturday, and I drove into town and then through town: Papa's house, the house where I grew up, was on the other side of the river. The rain spattered my windshield before I was halfway there, and I thought about waiting for another day.

But I went on.

It had been a late spring. Hillsides beside the road were brown, the grass plastered flat. In the woods beyond the hills you could see bare, wet hardwood among the firs. My wipers squeaked across the glass, and the tires made a sticky noise on the pavement. I shut the wipers off to see how hard it was coming down, but the water blurred my windshield and I snapped them back on fast.

The rain was falling into the river, and I crossed the bridge and following the curve out of town I passed my sister Sylvie's road and thought about when she had come to my place two days before. She had talked about Papa's house. Marie, my wife, had made an excuse and left the room: she didn't like Sylvie much. I had to listen, because she's my sister. She sat at the kitchen table, hair wet because she had run through the rain from her car.

Sylvie spoke to me every so often about the house. She knew it was hers in the will, and didn't want to wait until Papa passed on. Somebody might as well get something from the old place, she would say. It was ridiculous that that house had stayed empty for four years. It would keep better if somebody lived there.

"Why let it sit there empty?" she asked me. Her elbows were on the table and she moved one enough to lift the coffee cup. She stared at me, her eyes the same brown as our father's.

I shrugged.

She leaned forward. "In another four years that goddamn house will fall down. What good will it do anybody then?"

"How do you know it'll be four years?"

"He's still strong. You've talked to the doctors."

"You want him to cooperate, huh?"

"Don't give me that. You know how he feels, just like I do." She stared over the cup, knowing she was right. I knew it too. He didn't want to stick around, and would have gone right after out mother did, if it had been up to him. Maybe he tried, with the strokes. But he had tough old bones, with their own ideas about dying.

"You know we could use the money," Sylvie said.

That didn't make it right. It was Papa's house, he didn't want anybody else living there, and I wouldn't let her convince me different. When she left, she told me that if I was inheriting the house, I'd sell it for sure, but that wasn't the truth, not at all.

My wife came back into the room.

"I know she's your sister..."

"You don't have to say it."

Marie came over and sat down with me. "How was he today?"

I had been to visit. "Same as ever."

"Still not writing?"

"The pen and paper sit there on the table. He knows what you're saying, but won't lift a goddamn finger."

"Are you sure he knows?" she said.

"I'm sure."

"The poor man." Marie shook her head a little, pushed at her glasses. I was a late son, and then I got married a little late, so Papa was always old when Marie knew him, she never saw him in the little wooden boat, one hand on the outboard, le moteur, running down the river to the ocean, steering out the channel past Pound O' Tea island, squinting against the glare. He didn't like sunglasses, said they changed the color of things and he liked to see things the way they were. Even now, blind, he has the evidence: squint lines around his eyes.

"I wish you'd known him," I told Marie.

She made a sad smile, and I got up and looked out the window at the rain falling.

In ten minutes I took a left on Lambert Road. The house was a short distance away. It was still raining under a low gray sky. I parked in front of the shed and climbed the steps to the front door, went into the kitchen. Inside, I opened all the windows, and rain came in and speckled the dust on the sills. The house smelled damp, which reminded me of what Sylvie had said.

Upstairs in my old bedroom, I sat on the little bed and looked out the window, but couldn't see much of the yard because of the rain washing over the glass. On the shelf beside the bed were my old serial books: Tom Swift, The Rover Boys, The Army Boys. I remembered reading them in bed, late, with a flashlight, everything dark except me and my book. I took a book down and thumbed through it. Its pages were dry and the print seemed bigger than today's books.

Papa stopped printing his block-letter notes about six months before that. Until then, you could talk to him and he would print his answer. But he stopped. He had gotten grouchy and then he stopped writing. He got tired, I guess. The last thing he wrote was after I mentioned his blood count. I told him it was improved, and he wrote a note: BIG DEAL. He threw the felt-tip and pad on the floor, and hadn't written anything since. When I spoke to him, he pretended not to hear. All he did was lie in bed, he wouldn't talk to anybody. He'd wake up a little at mealtimes, though. He put on weight until it took two nurses to get him out of bed and into a wheelchair so they could push him to the dining room, and three to get him back into bed. I would help when I was there, and it was strange: he used to tuck me in when I was little, and now I was helping him.

I rolled out of my old bed, putting Tom Swift back

on the shelf. I checked out the upstairs, then went down to the living room and sat on the couch. Everything was familiar: the braided run my mother had made, the dark picture of an Indian sitting on a horse, sticking his arms into the air, that hung on the wall over the TV, the stack of National Geographics on the floor. Alone in the house I felt the past traveling away from me. I seemed too big for the small room. It made me nervous, and I got up and headed for the cellar door beside the stairway from my room.

The cellar was musty, like always. I felt around for the bulb, and saw the workbench and tools, the outboard on the pallet. I walked over, unlocked the cellar doors and shoved them open. The metal doors banged on the ground: there used to be a post for each of them, but they were gone.

Lifting the outboard made a twinge in my back, but it didn't seem serious, so I went ahead. But it seemed to gain weight every year. I staggered up the cement steps and through the rain to the barrel. There was scum on the water. I felt another twinge when I lifted the outboard into the barrel.

Back in the cellar, I cleaned the spark plug, brought it and the gas can outside to the barrel. By the time I had the motor running, my arm was dead tired from pulling the cord. It ran rough at first, as if it was cramped in the barrel, but after I set the mix the sound smoothed a little. I went inside to the kitchen and sat by a window watching the blue smoke rise through the rain, thinking that the outboard should have been on a boat in the water somewhere, instead of locked into the barrel.

Papa used to take me out in the boat. We'd run out
to one of the islands, trolling on the way. If we caught
something we'd eat it for lunch, cooking it in the frypan
over one of those wire grills you stick in the ground.
We'd burn driftwood and get a good fire going. I liked
to watch the blue and green flames in the burning
driftwood.

He didn't talk much even then, but he showed me
things. Once we got caught in a shower and he built a
lean-to with pine boughs and we sat underneath listening to the rain patter, watching the waves wash up on
the dead seaweed at the high-water mark, and the rain,
it didn't matter at all.

The wind shifted, and now the rain beat against the
window. I couldn't see the outboard. Thirty minutes had
passed; I went outside and cut the motor. It smelled
smoky in the rain. The water stopped boiling, and I
disconnected the fuel line from the can. When I lifted
the outboard over the edge of the barrel, the twinge was
sharper in my back, and I had to stop and hold my
breath. Then it went away, and I was careful carrying it
back to the cellar, easing it down onto the pallet. I went
back for the gas can, then locked the cellar. Upstairs,
after a last look around, I locked the windows shut, then
the side door. Back in my car, I headed off through the
downpour.

The next day it was still raining when we went to
visit. We ran across the parking lot between cars. Papa
wasn't in his room, so we walked through the big lobby
to the dining room, and saw him in his wheelchair,

feeling around on his plate and stuffing his food into his mouth. Sylvie sat beside him, guiding his fork hand, talking into his ear. I knew what she was saying: it was as plain on her face as the gravy on Papa's. When she saw us, she got a hard expression.

"Papa," I said loudly. "It's me and Marie."

He went on eating. I looked at Sylvie. "Any progress?"

"No," Sylvie said.

"He won't write, huh?"

She looked at the pad and pen on the table.

Papa was feeling around to see if he'd missed anything on his plate. A pretty nurse came over, said something in his ear and took his dishes away.

Papa sat back in the chair.

"Well, Daddy," Sylvie said, a hand on his shoulder. "I have to go. Robert's here. I'll see you tomorrow." She patted his shoulder; he didn't pay any attention. She said goodbye and left.

The nurse returned and cleaned him up with a washcloth.

"Would you like to go back to your room, Raymond?" she asked, pulling the chair back from the table. "We've tried the sitting room," she told me, "but he doesn't seem to want it."

Papa gave no sign he heard her. We walked beside them as she pushed the wheelchair through the corridor, chattering about what a sweetheart Dad was, how all the nurses loved him. "Aren't you a sweetheart, Raymond?" she cooed. Looking at me, she said, "The only thing we don't like is putting him back in bed." She laughed. "You've put on a little weight, haven't you dear?" Smiling brightly at me, she asked if I would help today.

"I'll help."

"Oh, good. Then we'll only need one more nurse." She stopped at the desk in the lobby, bringing another nurse along with us. We went into Papa's room, and she parked the chair next to the bed, locking the wheels. I moved the chair as the two nurses lifted him up by his arms, turned him and let his upper half down onto the mattress. I felt it in my back when I picked his legs up and swung them over. The back had been stiff all day, and I was careful when I straightened. The nurses rolled Papa over, tucked him in, and gave us a smile. Then they left.

I felt the small of my back with my fingertips.

Marie and I sat at the foot of the bed. Papa's head lay on the white pillow. I told him about my visit to the house, how I'd aired it, dusted the furniture, changed a couple of light bulbs. He just sat there until I mentioned the outboard. Then he did something with his head, a little movement, like he was cocking an ear.

Marie put a hand on my arm.

I described everything, from carrying it out of the cellar to putting the gas in, to the water boiling and the blue smoke rising. When I stopped, he held out his hands.

I smiled at Marie.

Papa struggled to sit up. He took the pad and pen from me and nodded his head. He wrote something and held the pad out. It said: BIG DEAL. I looked at Marie. Papa printed something else. He was pressing down hard on the paper. He turned it around, and I had to lean

close. He had written: GIVE HER LA DAMN
MAISON.

He ripped the paper off, crumpled it up and threw
it away. He bounced the pad and pen off the wall, then
lay back, real heavy. I couldn't look at him. I looked out
the window. It was still raining, the glass was blurred. I
listened to Papa breathing. Nobody said a word. We sat
there until my back began to ache.

Mackerel

Sanford Biggs sat on the desk-edge, watching his freshmen writing students scuff and clatter to their seats. To his left April sunshine streamed through the windows, illuminating dust that the students had set into motion.

The students took a long time to settle.

Biggs impatiently undid his gray ponytail, pulled it tighter, and slipped the elastic back into place. Finally he held a small magazine aloft and said, "We have spent nearly a semester discussing American literature as influenced by war."

The students looked warily at the magazine.

Biggs circled the desk, perched on the chair back, boots on the seat, a favorite posture. He let the magazine drop to the desk, then pressed his fingertips to his chin. "We've looked at Bierce and Crane, Hemingway and Cummings, Mailer and Jones. Most recently, my

dear students, you have spent precious time enjoying
the original M.A.S.H. and its portrayal of life in Ko-
rea."

This was how he talked to his students. They
glanced sideways at one another, while Biggs smiled. It
was so nice to get any kind of reaction from them. He
said, "Before we begin Mr. O'Brien's Going After
Cacciato, I have decided to change our tack a wee bit,
and share with you something from this modest example of the small press." He leaned forward precari-
ously, picked up the magazine, waved it at them. "So
far," he said, "all of our reading has been concerned
with the participants' point of view." There was a sound
from the back of the classroom, and Biggs peered at
one of the students. "Would you agree with that assess-
ment, Mr. Tolliver?"

A thin boy, wearing a bright green tropical shirt,
looked up at Biggs.

"Dean?"

"Uh, sure," Dean said. One of his neighbors
laughed.

"Very good, Mr. Tolliver," Biggs climbed down
from the chair, careful not to tip it over, walked around
the desk and sat on its front edge, ankles crossed. He
looked down at himself and was benignly pleased at the
way his fatigue pants pooched up in the front. After a
quick glance at the blonde who occupied the front left
corner seat (he thought of her as Front Left), he went
on. "As I was saying, today I believe we will look at
something a little different. Something about war from
a different perspective. Do you think that will be all
right?"

Dean Tolliver shrugged with some bravado and said, "Sure."

"Very fine." Biggs held the magazine out, spoke to the class at large. "In another break with tradition, perhaps we'll let Mr. Tolliver honor us with a reading."

"Aw, Mr. Biggs."

"Mr. Tolliver," Biggs said. "I would like to know that on at least one occasion, your entire attention was focused on the subject at hand." He waited until Dean reluctantly rose from his seat and slouched to the front. Then he opened the magazine, folded the title page back, handed it to him. "Begin."

Dean cleared his throat. He looked down at the story and started to read.

On the day of the first draft lottery, Mark Nolan and I cut all our classes and went fishing. We knew the mackerel were running, had seen the kids hauling them in from the State Pier a couple of blocks away from my Old Port apartment. Mark had just moved in with me: I'd lost one roommate and had gotten his name off the cafeteria corkboard two weeks before.

We were just getting to know one another.

It was a nice day, the sky clear and deep blue, the kind of sky that makes you think of changes. We sat on the old wharf behind the warehouse, on the narrow part that borders the back of the wooden building. The sun shone through the cool air and the building held its heat against us. It was noisy on the waterfront, the water choppy. We could see the mackerel moving through the water, swimming in unison like some sort of underwater mobile just below the surface. The school would go

out of sight but we knew where they were by the distur-
bance they caused. You cast ahead of them and let them
swim up to the lure. If one struck, you hauled him in,
disengaged him from the hook and broke his back on
the beam. Then he went into the green trash bag. Sometimes they swam by close and you could see the whole
thing.

The seagulls spotted us before long and a couple
of them hung around, perched atop the pilings, swinging off to fly in front of us, holding steady into the
breeze. One of them came up close as I took a mackerel
off the hook and I tossed him the gristle and he flew off
and swallowed it. I put the fish in the green bag. It
flopped around in there, slapping against the plastic.

By noon we had enough for a meal and we put our
gear down and lit cigarettes and sat looking at the boats.
The tide was coming in and I could hear the waves
slapping around beneath the planking. I had brought
some wine, and I peeled the metallic wrapping off and
took a corkscrew from my pocket, which made Mark
laugh.

"What were they," he said, "out of Old Duke?"

I imitated his voice: "No, they weren't out of Old
Duke." I stabbed the corkscrew in, twisted it until it was
seated, put the bottle between my knees and yanked the
cork out. "This is no time to worry about expense.
What is it they say? 'Eat, drink and be merry, for tomorrow you may die.'"

Mark said, "You'll jinx us."

"I'm lucky." I said this hoping it might prove true.
Actually, I had neither a lucky nor a particularly unlucky history.

"I'm not," Mark said.

"Who says?"

He shrugged. "I'm just not."

"You caught some fish, didn't you?"

"That just means the fish were unlucky."

I laughed, handed him the bottle. He drank and passed it back.

"I'll get a low one tonight," he said, "you wait and see."

"So then they find something wrong with you. Think positive."

Mark shook his head.

"Join the Coast Guard."

"I got a bad eye."

"They won't take you?"

"I checked it out already."

"But the army will?"

"I'm breathing, aren't I?"

We sat there until the wine was gone, then tied the trash bag off and took it back to the apartment on Danforth Street. We had to get the place ready for a party. All our friends were coming over to get drunk and watch the lottery numbers come up. Either you'd be celebrating or drowning your sorrows.

It would work out regardless.

There was still one fish alive in the bag, and every few steps it would flop halfheartedly, and after a while Mark wouldn't carry the bag any more. He said it gave him the creeps.

So I took it the rest of the way home.

We drank while we made nachos and iced down two coolers of beer, and Mark went out for more wine before we finished. He came back with a third of the bottle gone: he'd drank out of the paper bag like a wino as he'd walked through the Old Port. He grinned and brushed the hair off his forehead when I held the bottle up and looked at it.

"Sure you don't mind if I have some?" I said.

"Just don't drink it all."

I punched his shoulder and he laughed, staggering a little.

We moved the desk out of my room and into a corner of the living room, and put Mark's TV on it. It was an old house with big rooms with high ceilings and wide-planked floors. We turned on the news and, as we hauled chairs in from our bedrooms, watched the latest footage. There was apparently some heavy fighting going on. They showed corpsmen dragging casualties behind sandbagged positions.

"Appropriate," Mark said, standing in the middle of the room, hands on his hips, staring at the TV. "Put you right in the mood for it."

"Take it easy," I said.

He laughed, shook his head.

I stopped to watch, too, felt my stomach clench at the images.

The others began arriving soon and by eight o'clock it was noisy and smoky and all the chairs were occupied. I was sitting on the couch with Mark on one side and my girlfriend Jody on the other. Jody, nervous for me but in no personal danger, had gone to her classes that day.

The production began with some guy talking about fair play and equality. We listened closely, everybody tense with the exception of Mark Nolan, who was too far along to be tense. He was leaning back, peering through half-closed eyes at the television screen. He saw me looking at him and lifted his latest bottle in a sort of salute. Then he took a gulp. Mark didn't do dope and ignored the joints circulating the room, but a bottle couldn't get past him.

"Be over soon," I said to him.

"What I'm afraid of," he said.

"You got to have confidence."

"I told you about my luck."

Just then one of the guys from school stood up, reeling a bit, and held his hands in the air. It was Rick Dunham, one of the lesser campus radicals. "Your attention please," he said. His rimless glasses were slightly askew. He held a joint in his fingers.

"Move it, Dunham," someone said.

"First, a few words," Dunham said. He took a long toke, held his breath, let it out. "Ladies and gentlemen," he said, gesturing toward the TV, "we are gathered together to witness the joining of this man, Uncle Sam, and this woman, Liberty, in the bonds of holy rape!" He weaved a little on his feet.

"Shut up," someone suggested.

"What politics hath joined together, let no man tear asunder!" Dunham said. Then a hand reached up and pulled him down to the floor. This was accomplished quite easily due to his reduced state of balance. When he was out of the way we were shocked to see the slow-moving lines of dates and numbers on the screen.

"It's started!"

"Dunham, you ass!"

Jim Nichols

"Quiet!"

I took a quick look at Mark, saw that he had passed out on the couch, head forward, chin on his chest. I pried the wine bottle out of his fist and set it on the floor, then looked back at the TV. There was no noise now except the scratch of Jody's pencil as she took down the numbers.

It was high drama. We drank and smoked quietly but seriously and every now and then someone would comment as his number came up. At first the comments were obscene, then we moved into the gray area of the two hundreds, where you didn't know for sure that you'd be drafted. My own birthday wasn't selected until near the end. I was number 318, and I felt the knot in my stomach disolve.

Mark was still asleep. I didn't know his birthday.

People were standing up, putting on jackets, chattering. There were fifteen or twenty kids there.

"What was yours?" I asked Jody.

"Twenty-five. I'm glad they wasted it on me."

Kids were saying goodnight, banging through the doorway into the hall, stomping down the stairs. Pretty soon everyone was gone but Dunham. He lay passed out on the floor. He and Mark were the only casualties. I covered them with blankets and left them where they'd fallen: Jody and I were high and happy and too anxious to get to bed and celebrate my high number to deal with them. After, we held each other and I said, "What if I'd gotten a low one?"

"You could refuse."

"And go to jail."

"There's Canada."

"Jesus," I said.

We slept late but still were the first ones up. Dunham hadn't moved, was still lying on the floor, holding the blanket around himself, snoring with his mouth open, the only body in sight, surrounded by the scattered debris of the party. Mark had evidently roused himself enough to get to bed at some point during the night. There were bottles and ashtrays everywhere. The floor was sticky and there were roaches on the windowsills. Chairs were knocked over, blankets and pillows scattered, pictures hanging crooked, lamps lying in sticky pools of wine.

"I'm not tackling this without a shower," Jody said.

I followed her to the bathroom. When we got back to the living room Dunham was sitting on the couch looking at the sheet of paper where Jody had copied down the dates.

"What does 225 get you?" he said.

"Depends," I said.

"On what?"

"Tricky Dick."

He stood up and groaned, straightening his glasses with two hands.

We heard a door open and turned to see Mark standing in his bedroom doorway, dressed as he'd been last night, hair sticking out, whiskery and red-eyed.

"You look good," I said.

"You're funny." He came haltingly into the room, clawed his hair out of his eyes, looked at Dunham. "That the results?"

"Yup."

"How'd you do?"

"225," Dunham said.

"How about you?"

I told him and he shook his head.

"When's your birthday, Marcus?" Dunham said.

Mark told him, looked around, picked a chair up off the floor, straddled it. "Go ahead," he said. "Tell me the good news."

Dunham scanned the sheet of paper, looked puzzled, held it closer. Then he let out a laugh.

"What's so funny?" Mark said.

"Marcus," Dunham said, "you're quite a guy."

Mark held his hand out for the paper.

Dunham grinned at me. "He almost won the damn thing."

Mark dropped the sheet of paper on the floor and went back into his room without a word. He shut the door quietly.

Dunham looked at Mark's door. "I guess I shouldn't have laughed. Tell him I'm sorry, will you?" He looked around for his jacket and left. Jody and I started picking up, and by the time Mark came back, still not speaking but pitching in, we were well along with it. With his help, in another hour things were pretty much back to normal.

"How about some breakfast?" I said. "How about those fish?" We had cleaned them and cut their heads off so all I had to do was wrap them in tin foil, salt and pepper and lemon-juice them and start them broiling in the gas stove. I love fish for breakfast, and soon the smell was making me hungry. I made a pot of coffee and brought the fish and the coffee to the table. We sat

down and ate, peeling the skin, picking the soft gray
flesh off the bones. Jody ate all the crisp tails. It wasn't
bad. We put the dishes in the sink and the bones and
scrap into the green trash bag we'd kept the fish in. I
stuffed some newspaper on top of the debris and tied
the bag and put it in the wastebasket.

Then I joined the other two on the couch.

Mark looked at me and shook his head.

"Dunham said he's sorry," I told him.

"Dunham's the least of my worries."

"Maybe something will happen," Jody said.

Mark sighed. We sipped the hot coffee. I fetched
the pot and refilled the cups, then opened the windows
for the fresh, salty air.

"That's better," Jody said.

We sat on the couch, feeling the breeze.

"I can still smell those goddamn fish," Mark said.
He went to the wastebasket and pulled the trash bag
out. It ripped on a broken bottle and some of the fish
scraps fell out at his feet. He started laughing. Jody and
I looked at each other. Mark held the torn bag up and
swore. He kicked at the pieces of dead fish and threw
the bag hard into the basket.

"Hey, take it easy," I said.

"Sorry." He knelt to pick up the mess, flipping the
pieces of fish into the trash. His hands went down to his
thighs and he shook his head and sat back on his heels.
I didn't know what to say to him. I was just getting to
know him. The wind blew in through the open windows
and rattled the paper shades. But it couldn't get rid of
the smell of the dead fish.

"The end," Dean Tolliver said. He handed the

magazine back to Biggs, stuffed his hands into his pockets and walked back to his one-piece desk.

"Thank you, Dean. You did that quite well."

Dean smirked, burnished his fingernails on his bright green shirt.

"Any comments?" Biggs asked.

"Vietnam," Front Left said.

"Correct!" Biggs said. "Very good, dear."

"I knew it," she said to the girl beside her. Biggs waited, but no one else had anything to contribute. He sighed, looked around at them. No one allowed him to meet their eyes. He shook his head. They were really quite a remarkable class. They would all write something about war, because it was this semester's assignment. Then they would go back to their stories about divorce, or grandparents in nursing homes, or committing suicide because no one understood them. He glanced at the clock over the door, saw that the period was only half over and supressed another sigh. Tapping the magazine against his leg, he walked around the desk, perched atop the chair, surveyed the class.

"Dean," he said then.

Dean rolled his eyes. "What?"

"What did you think of the story, Dean? Truthfully, now. Did any of it strike you?"

"The part about cutting classes wasn't bad."

Biggs waited until the students stopped laughing. "The boy in the story," he said. "What do you suppose happened to him?"

"How would I know?" Dean said.

"Think about it."

"I suppose he finished picking up the fish."

"Then?"

"Why are you asking me?"

Biggs kept staring at him.

"All right," Dean said. "I suppose he got drafted."

"And after that?"

"It doesn't say."

"Are there no clues?"

Dean was staring back at Biggs now. "No."

"None at all?"

The rest of the class was quiet.

"Maybe," Dean said.

"All right," Biggs said. "The boy in the story died. He was drafted, went to Vietnam and was killed. He left not long after the party and the narrator of the story never saw him again."

Dean shifted uneasily in his seat.

"Ergo," Biggs said, "he wound up in his own green bag."

"You can't say that for sure," Dean said.

"Oh yes I can," Biggs said. "I wrote the damn story."

Dean kept his eyes on Biggs. The other students looked at their desks. Biggs sat with with his chin in his hands and his elbows on his knees, waiting, but nobody said anything. After a minute or two he told them they were dismissed, and the students gathered their things and quickly the room emptied. Tolliver was the last one, and he paused at the door for a quick look back at Biggs. Then he left.

Biggs got down from the chair and went to the window. The sunlight was warm and toasty. He could see the students as they burst out of the building, ahead of the bell, free from thought. To get to the cafeteria they had to walk through the quadrangle in the center of the campus, and Biggs watched them pass the upsloped corner where, in his day, they had always put the speakers' platforms. There were twenty-five students and they flowed past the corner and around a curve toward the next brick building, and Biggs could see Dean Tolliver's green shirt among them, sparkling in the sunlight, moving in near-unison with the rest.

Loons

I stop rowing and swing the little oars up to rest on the black swell of the rubber dinghy. Immediately, the light breeze begins pushing us gently toward the cabin where Kate is staying. There's a light over the door of her cabin and we float along the wrinkled line of its reflection. It's warm, the air damp: rain has fallen four of the five days we've been at this camp. Today, toward dinner-time, it finally stopped and now, though still overcast, it's mild and quiet on the lake. But the overcast makes it very dark.

Kate is facing me, knees together, hands between her thighs. My legs flank hers in the small craft and, leaning toward one another, our faces are only inches apart.

"Isn't this nice?" I say.

"Mmmm."

"I wonder where the loons went to?"

"Maybe they were waiting for you to stop rowing."

In the lodge at the opposite end of the camp, where we were sitting around the rough-hewn table talking with the others, we were able to hear the loons calling to each other across the lake. Every few minutes, someone would say, "Listen!" and the room would go quiet. But since we pushed off from the dock there have been none of the eerie cries. Now there's just the wind ruffling through the treetops on the shore and the water licking the rubber dinghy.

"They sounded so heartbroken," Kate whispers now.

We're getting close to the rocks near the cabin, and I take the oars and row us back out into the lake. Then I put up the oars. The breeze starts nudging us shoreward again. We've gone back and forth several times in this way since rowing across the cove along which the camps are situated.

The cove cuts deeply into the wooded shoreline.

"I wonder why they sound so lonely," Kate says.

We sit quietly, listening. But the loons aren't cooperating.

"Do loons mate for life?" I say then. "Like geese?"

"I don't know."

"That might explain it."

She raises her eyebrows.

"Maybe the ones we hear don't have anyone yet," I say with a little laugh.

She considers it. "Maybe."

"Sure. They wouldn't be out there calling if they had someone. They'd be sitting at home with their feet up."

"Unless," she says, "they were unhappily married."

"And out philandering," I say.

"Right." She laughs, aware that we're making fun of our hesitant new relationship, misquoting some of our increasingly intimate conversations. Then she's quiet, and we listen for the cries, but for the moment there are no single or philandering loons in evidence on the lake.

"Aw," I say, "they probably just like making a noise."

She turns to look at the cabin, to see how close we are, shifting her weight, rocking us a little. She turns back, gives me a wry half-smile, reaches for my hands. "Is this all right?" she says. "To hold hands?"

"I think so." I feel her thumbs moving over mine.

"We don't want to be philandering loons."

"No," I say. "We don't want that."

"You're happily married."

"Right," I say. "You, too."

"Exactly."

We smile at each other.

"I'm still glad I didn't row back alone," she says.

I'm glad too, although at the lodge earlier, when she yawned and said it was time for her to go, it was my intention to let her do just that: it was the last night and she could go back to her cabin and I could stay where I was and there would be no harm done and no familial promises broken.

Obviously: the smart thing to do.

But then she looked back at me from the door and I was suddenly unable to let her just walk (or row) away. I was unable to dismiss our five-day intimacy so easily. "You want some company?" I blurted.

One of the older ladies at the workshop smiled.

Kate looked down at her hand on the latch, then up at me.

"Sure," she said.

We smiled at one another, tempting fate, giving ourselves a last opportunity to misbehave. Which didn't mean necessarily that we would misbehave. I still planned on doing the grown-up thing. I just couldn't let her go without a proper goodbye.

I'd decided six months before, on my birthday, that I was going to grow up. This year I was forty, and by some good fortune still had a family, and I'd decided to have no more affairs. I let my wife in on it, too, telling her that I was going to treat this birthday as a bench-mark, as the start of my grown-up existence. I was done playing around, I was going to stop acting like an adolescent every time a pretty girl came by, I was going to stop flirting before it got me into even worse trouble than I already was in. (I had to pretend, in order to talk this way, that the little unconsumated affair she'd discovered, the afore-mentioned trouble, was the worst thing I'd ever done.)

I was completely serious, too, aware of how close I'd come to ruining it all. It was pure good luck that nothing had actually happened, that I could truthfully state that I'd been only headed toward disaster. Because it was the truth (this time), I was able to convince my wife that I hadn't made love to the girl. Certain portions of her letter (I still couldn't believe she'd sent me a letter, and that my wife had chosen that day to stay home from work), portions that spoke of how nice it would be when we finally, etc., while making it impossible to disguise my intentions, did prove that I hadn't carried them out yet.

Which allowed my wife to forgive me.

But it was a very close thing, and I promised both myself and my wife that I was going to take our marriage more seriously. We had ten years in and two children, after all.

It was time.

"I'm a married man," I said, taking my wife's hands. It was a little like declaring at an AA meeting, but never mind that, I meant what I said. And six months later, I went off to this workshop still full of resolve. This would be my first real test. If I could get through one of these, I could get through anything. I hedged a little by hoping all the women would be plain, or Lesbians, but when it turned out that that was asking too much, I thought: All right, we'll do it the hard way. I still wanted to be good. And there was no reason I couldn't, even if the first woman I saw, this Kate, happened to look like Lauren Bacall in To Have and Have Not.

Kate's long hands come farther into mine, and our fingers move together, a quick dry sound against the soft noise of the lake. The breeze pushes us in toward the cabin. We sit still until I can hear the water splashing on the rocks and then I let go of her hands and take the oars and row us out again, farther this time, out past where the two points pinch the cove off from the rest of the lake.

She shifts her weight and I feel her feet under me, beneath the plastic bench seat. I ship the little oars, wondering if she knows what she's doing. Her feet send a signal through the plastic into my center, and then on up through my body.

We listen for the loons. But it's still quiet.

"I loved the story you read today," she says then.

"Did you?"

"It was funny," she says, "but kind of sad, too."

"I like to touch all the bases."

She breathes a little laughter, then says, "Has your wife ever had an affair?"

"Not that I know of."

"That was completely made up?"

I nod.

Kate sighs.

"How about you?" I say after a little while. "Has your spouse ever...?" I speak in a slightly mocking way, as I can't help doing whenever I talk to a woman about another man.

"Oh, I don't think so."

"Oh," I say.

We sit drifting. The breeze moves us back into the cove, toward her cabin, scattering the reflected light on the water, and we talk about writing, praising each other's work, the stuff we read to the group over the course of the week. Then we talk about how nice it has been, getting to know one another, becoming friends, and how unlucky that we each have someone already.

"In a perfect world..." I say.

"Yes." She knows the rest: we've said it often enough these past few days.

"It's too bad we're so honorable," I say.

She smiles a little. "I don't feel very honorable."

Our faces are still close and when she says that I lean forward to kiss her.

But she whispers, "Don't."

I pull back, surprised, then grateful. I forgot myself there for a moment. She has such a pretty mouth, it's only natural to want to kiss her.

"I don't want to just start in," she says.

"Right," I say, nodding. I understand. We have agreed that we should be rational about it. We don't want one kiss to lead to another and so on. If anything's going to happen, despite our good intentions, we want it to have been decided upon. We don't want it to be simply giving in. All this stuff is so damn complicated, but she is smart and articulate about it, as she is about everything we've discussed. I knew she would be the first time I saw her. You could see it in her eyes. Even more: you could see it in the way she carried herself. She stood out from the rest of them from day one, from the time I drove into the little camp, up to the cabin they'd assigned me.

My cabin was next to the lodge, and there was a group of them standing on the lodge's dock, looking out at the cove, admiring the setting of the workshop. (That first day was sunny and warm, the nicest day of the whole week.)

They all turned to peer at the new arrival.

I got out of the car and walked over, passing the log-cabin lodge, joining them on the dock, and she was the striking one, tall and with that nice carriage and, as I got closer, that smart look in her eyes.

I smiled at her, then remembered about being good and turned away to introduce myself around: there were a couple of older ladies, their handshakes dry and perfunctory, and a blonde, very pretty girl (with whom I felt no kinship whatever), some younger and not so pretty ones, a rather frail-looking older man and another guy about my own age who was standing next to Kate and who'd been chatting her up I approached.

He shook hands grudgingly, and stuck his chin in the air.

I turned to Kate and took her hand.

She smiled into my eyes and the connection was made. I realized it at once. Of course, I told myself, there were always going to be connections and opportunities. The trick was to not act on them. It was the same thing I'd told my wife, when she'd wondered whether it was very smart to be going off alone to a workshop in the boonies. You couldn't isolate yourself from temptation, I told her. That's why going to this workshop was a good idea. It would allow me to prove to myself that I'd changed.

And so far it had all worked out. Nothing untoward had occurred. Oh, Kate and I were drawn to each other, there's no denying that. And we did start sitting together, during the readings, and eating together, and on the third and fourth days, it's true, we visited back and forth in the evening, lighted fires in the crumbling old fireplaces and started talking about friendship, and wondering how intimate one could be without betraying a trust, and I admit that we had discussions in which we found ourselves wondering just how often you met

someone whose spirit seemed kindred, and we did hug
on one occasion when, quite late on the fourth night,
after we'd finished off a bottle of wine, I got up to head
back to my own cabin. (I figured a little hug wouldn't
hurt anything, and she obviously thought the same,
from the way she accompanied me to the door and put
her hand on my arm.)

But that had been the extent of it, the week had
passed without a major moral failure, and we were still
uncorrupted when the last night came, the night when
everyone walked or rowed to the lodge to drink and say
goodbye, the night before we all went home, the night
that found us alone eventually in the dinghy on the lake.

This time after I row us out past the points (listening for the loons, who still aren't calling; I wonder
what in hell they are waiting for), we can see flashlights
on the side of the cove by the lodge. Some of the lights
bob off through the brush, and others come shining
down to the lake. Voices carry across the water to the
rubber raft. There is laughter, and the splashes and
hollow sounds of people getting into boats.

"Looks like the party's over," I say.

"It must be getting late."

"Maybe we'd better go in, too?"

"I suppose."

I turn the dinghy, begin rowing slowly in toward
the dock, wondering if she will start something. That
will be the last difficulty we might have. I don't think
I'll start anything. That possibility has been postponed
for so long, while we rowed back and forth, that I think
I can be good now out of sheer inertia. I'm glad we've

spent this time together, though, glad I didn't let her go off alone. It's much more pleasant to say goodbye this way.

I take my time rowing in. Neither of us says anything. The flashlights disappear one by one on the shore, and the other boats all make it in before we do.

I hold the dinghy against the wood while she steps out. Then I follow, and stand beside her, holding the painter. Little waves blow under the dock and onto the rocks. I walk the dinghy up the dock to the shore. "Are you any good at tying knots?" I say.

"No."

I loop the line around the curving trunk of a tree growing out of the bank next to the dock. I hitch it twice, let it fall. "That'll have to do."

We walk the little pine-needled path to her cabin, climb the three steps up to the porch.

I take her hands.

She catches her breath.

I give a little tug and she comes into my arms.

Overhead, as I hold her, there are tiny sounds, moths throwing themselves against the porch light. I feel her hair on my cheek. I don't say anything. It's hard to breathe, let alone speak. After another moment I put my knuckle under her chin and nudge her head back. She's waiting, eyes closed, and next to the reality of her body, her pretty mouth, my resolve vanishes.

Just as I lean to kiss her, the loons start in.

When the first one cries out, throwing its wild song over the lake, Kate and I both jump. Kate's eyes blink open and she looks up at me, her eyes moving.

A second long call rises, trills, descends.

The first answers.

Then they're singing together, louder than I've ever heard them. Their cries - echoing back and forth across the lake, rising and falling in turn, competing, deranged - send shivers through me.

"My God," Kate says. "I thought they were gone."

"They were there all along."

The birds keep it up. We listen for a long time. Then, finally, they start to subside. I turn to Kate and our lips come naturally together, and it's as sad and warm as I would have expected. After a time she reaches behind her for the door and pulls it open, and I hold onto her as we maneuver ourselves inside and over to the little sofa by the fireplace.

We sit entwined, looking at each other. The light from the porch filters in through cloth curtains over the little windows. Her eyes shine.

I manage a smile, and she sighs a little laughter.

Outside, the loons call softly from the lake.

Slow Monkeys

This skinny kid's sitting across from me when Bartlett shuffles into the room, looking rough: eyes bloodshot, hair all sticking up and sneaker laces trailing along behind. Gray sweaty whiskers. The kid stares, then looks away.

"Where you been?" I ask.

Bartlett's barely got enough energy to shrug.

It's not like I can't guess, though.

The Salvation Army man comes into the room then, plops his bible down on the end of the table, holds it open with his palms. His head almost touches the drop-ceiling and he's skinny as a flagpole. He wears these black vests. I call him Ichabod Crane to myself because he reminds me of a drawing I saw in a book when I was a kid. Long neck; big Adam's Apple.

"Gentlemen," the Salvation Army man says.

We bow our heads. I feel my throat bunch up

under my chin and, like always when I notice I'm fat, I feel separated from the rest of them. Everybody else these days is skinny except Elmore, who isn't exactly fat and who isn't around today anyway. Of course even if there was another blimp around, I wouldn't hang with him and get laughed at, like those two fatties on the mini-bikes you see posters of.

No sir.

"If the clouds be full of rain," the S.A. man says, "they empty themselves upon the earth. And if the tree falleth toward the south, or toward the north, in the place where the tree falleth, there it shall be." He clears his throat and flips through the pages. "Let us pray," he says, and starts in. We don't join him but when he stops we say, "Amen."

"Enjoy your meal, gentlemen."

The S.A. man takes off and we go up to the window and get a white-bread sandwich, a plastic cup of soup, a carton of milk from the old woman in the kitchen. We go back to the table and the kid opens the sandwich and looks inside.

"I wouldn't," I say.

The kid closes the sandwich fast. We all start eating. I ask Bartlett again where he's been and he answers this time, he says, "The usual." The food's helping him out. We take our dishes back and slide them through the window and the old woman who works for Ichabod puts them in the washer. The washer grinds and splashes. We sit down again until the S.A. man comes back to lead us along the hall to the Evening room. When we get there the kid hesitates at the door.

"I don't know about this," he says.

The S.A. man says, "I'm afraid we don't open our front door until morning."

"You mean I'm stuck?"

"It seems to work best," old Ichabod Crane says.

The kid comes into the room, looks around at the double row of cots, Christ pictures on the walls, the long scratched-up table with folding chairs around it.

Bartlett and I go to the table and sit. I watch the kid but he doesn't know it because when I squint a little my eyes sort of disappear and you can't tell where I'm looking. I see the kid decide to join us. He's early twenties, northern-sounding, scrawny. I don't know what he's doing at Sal's, but we ain't had much chance to talk: he came in just before Bartlett, kind of shy, looking around.

Bartlett points at my pocket. I fish a cigarette out and hand it over. We aren't supposed to smoke in here but Ichabod has given up trying to stop us and has put a tin ashtray on the table so we won't burn the place down. We light up and Bartlett starts rolling the tip against the ashtray. When it's a perfect little red cone, he takes a couple drags. Then he rolls it again. He opens his mouth and clears his throat, real shallow so he won't start coughing.

"So you had to go back," I say.

He rolls his big eyes over toward the kid, then back toward me. He's got a few hundred more wrinkles than when I saw him last.

"More treatment?"

"I'm scheduled," Bartlett says.

He's got the lung cancer, see: we might lose him.

I can see the kid thinking and after a little while he squares himself up and grins at us and holds out his hand. He says he's from Maine and his name is Barry. He has jet-black hair and is trying to grow a mustache. He can't be more than eighteen or nineteen. He looks us in the eye when he shakes our hands. Bartlett sits up a little straighter. "Now, are you on the road, Barry?" he says.

Barry likes the sound of that. "I guess you could say."

"And what precipitated...?"

Bartlett's getting high-falutin', so I know he's feeling better. Maybe he isn't as sick as I thought. Maybe he just needs a drink, I'm thinking, and I'm wondering how long it'll take before he tells the kid his story.

"Oh, I got fed up," the kid says. He goes on to tell us how he got tired of living at home, milking cows and shoveling shit, and he and his old man had a beef about putting on the storm windows and he just lit out and ended up here. He always wanted to be a writer, he says, and he figured he might as well bum around and find something to write about.

Bartlett's ears prick up at this. "And how are you liking it?" he says.

"It's different," the kid says.

I laugh and Bartlett rumbles a cough around in his chest. Then the S.A. man comes into the room and tells us we have five minutes. "Good night, gentlemen," he says, and pulls the door shut.

We move to the cots. The kid takes out a little notebook and a stub of a pencil. I laugh, he grins over at me and keeps writing. I lie down carefully on the cot so it won't break under me. I turn on my side so nothing will back up into my throat while I sleep. It's happened a few times. It's scary as hell to wake up like that.

Pretty soon the lights blink out. Then Bartlett starts wheezing. All the stuff in his lungs settles when he lies down. He doesn't want to really start coughing so he lets these wheezes stretch out and not quite finish. They get longer and longer until he finally starts coughing anyway, and then I ease myself out of my cot and go over to his and pound him on the back until the gunk shifts around to where he can stop.

Then after a while he dozes off.

It's still dark when the S.A. man opens the door. "Rise and shine, gentlemen," he says. He stands there in his black pants and vest, his white shirt, with his finger-tips together. "One note before breakfast," he says. "I've been advised that the Willis Orchard truck will be stopping by for any of you who might wish to pick today." He clops off down the hall.

We get scrambled eggs, grits and toast for break-fast. The kid takes one taste of his grits and spits it out.

"Make a note of that," I say.

The kid laughs.

We finish eating and drink a couple watery cups of coffee and talk about picking. Bartlett says he's broke and I say I am, too.

"That makes three of us," the kid says.

When we get outside the truck's waiting. I help Bartlett into the flat-bed and climb up after him, chafing my gut on the metal edge, wondering how I stay fat without any money. The driver is talking to Ichabod by the door. He laughs, pushes his Stetson higher.

The S.A. man laughs like a schoolgirl, hand on his mouth. They chew the fat until the sun has pushed up over the neighborhood and steam is coming off the street. Then the driver swings up into his truck and starts the engine.

We sit there looking down at the kid.

"It's worth a few dollars," Bartlett says, and I know he wants to tell his story. The kid says, "What the hell," throws his pack up and climbs in just as the truck starts moving.

We ride out into the country. At first it's scrub and hardpan, but then the groves appear and there are rows of orange trees on both sides of the road, people in the rows, hampers and crates and ladders. There are sprinklers fanning water about, rainbows in the air. We turn down a wide aisle and park in a clearing and the driver is out and walking before the engine has stopped deiseling. He leads us over to a man with his foot up on a crate. Then he walks off, adjusting his hat.

We stand in front of this sunburned guy.

"You boys feel like working?" he says.

"Yes sir," Bartlett says.

"Had anything to drink?"

"We been in the mission all night."

"All right," the man says. The driver comes back and the overseer tells him to find us a place to work. The driver nods to him, starts walking. We follow him down the big aisle and into a side row and up to a tree. "Start here," he says. "Move off that way. When you fill up the bin come get me and I'll find you another section. Don't eat the oranges on the trees. You can eat the ones on the ground if you want."

He turns around and walks off.

We start in. Bartlett and the kid do the climbing: I'm way too heavy for these little trees. Bartlett looks weightless on the ladder, like he could take another step from the top and just keep going up. They throw the oranges down onto the spongy grass and I crate them and take the crates to the hamper and throw them in. We fill one bin and the kid trots off to find the driver. They come back and we get going on another patch. All around us are these families picking. They are like something out of The Jungle Book, like monkeys moving through the forest, half seen, chattering. We are no different, only slower.

We're the slow monkeys.

When the sun gets high overhead the driver comes back and tells us to take a break. We sit down in the shade and Bartlett starts coughing. I whack his back for him until he stops. I hand him an orange from the hamper and he digs a thumb in and starts peeling and the rind-smell cuts through the air. Bartlett eats it like an apple and gets his chin all shiny. He looks over at the kid, who's lying down with his knees up.

I roll onto my side. "You gonna tell him, Bart?"

Bartlett shrugs. But I know he wants to.

The kid turns his head. "Tell me what?"

"About old Bart's TV show," I say.

Bartlett finishes off the orange, wipes his hands on his pants and his chin on his sleeve. He coughs a little, trying out his lungs, and they seem to be holding up for the moment.

"You had a TV show?" the kid says.

"Tell him," I say, because I know he's dying to.

"He doesn't want to hear all that."

"Oh yes I do," the kid says.

Bartlett sighs and pretends to give in. "It was a children's show," he says. "You know, they come on as guests and get milk and cookies? Every little city has one." He says all this carefully, as if he's only allowed a certain amount of breath for each word.

"We had one called Captain Lloyd's," the kid says.

"Exactly," Bartlett says. "I was called, ah, Stumpy Sparrow." He laughs a little, like he wishes he'd been called Captain Lloyd instead. "I wore a costume, did tricks for the kids," he says. "The studio put three big Ss over my door. I would pick out children from the mail they sent in." He sighs: a soft, clicky sound. "And they would send me around to grocery store openings and such. Once they hired a helicopter. It was hot in my costume in the helicopter. We went to an amusement park that had water slides and all that and I got my feathers wet."

He goes quiet, then, remembering.

"Tell him what happened." I give the kid a look so he'll pay attention. But I needn't have.

Bartlett sighs, nods. "On my show, the Stumpy Sparrow Show, there was a pigeon."

"A girl," I say.

The kid looks at me.

"A girl," Bartlett says, "dressed as a pigeon."

"Little girl or a big girl?" the kid says.

"A woman," Bartlett says.

"And there was a cat." I know my lines.

"A man," Bartlett says.

"Dressed like a cat?" the kid chimes in.

"Now you got it," I say.

Bartlett sits there with his little legs out in front of him and his hands in his lap. There's grime in the creases in his face and his eyes bug out and his hair is all over the place. He doesn't look like any TV star, and I see the kid wondering. But he's thinking he's stumbled onto something pretty interesting, too. He's not taking notes, to be polite, but he's reminding himself to later on. He keeps touching the shirt pocket that has the notebook.

"So what happened?" the kid says.

Bartlett hangs his head.

"The pigeon and the cat," I say, "they ran off together."

Bartlett's head hangs lower.

"He was in love with the pigeon," I say, "and she ran off with the fucking cat."

After a moment the kid says, "I'm sorry."

Bartlett rolls his eyes up toward the sky.

"That was the end of it," I say.

Bartlett nods. "I hadn't the will to go on."

"Or the cast," I say.

Bartlett smiles at the kid. When he smiles you can see that maybe he was once a pretty good-looking little guy. Then he gets a surprised look on his face and starts coughing. A piece of orange flies out of him. He bends over and is hacking raggedly and the guy who's in charge of us picks that moment to come walking up through the trees.

"He okay, or what?" he says.

Bartlett clenches his teeth.

"If he's sick get him out of here."

Bartlett starts in again, these deep barks that shake him. He covers his mouth, holds the other hand up. The guy watches him, then says, "Get him out of here." He walks over to look into the bin, then checks a little notebook like the kid's. "Go tell Willie to give you nine dollars," he says. "I'll have one of the boys drive you back." He looks at the kid. "You can work with somebody else," he says. "You're a pretty good climber."

The kid says, "Thanks anyway."

The guy shrugs, walks off.

They drive us back to town and we pool our money for a bucket of Church's Fried Chicken and a jug of wine. Bartlett's cough hasn't come back and he's doing all right, and I'm wondering whether he started himself coughing to get out of working the rest of the day. You can't tell sometimes with him.

But I don't care.

We cross under Kennedy and walk a couple of blocks to a vacant lot and sit on a telephone pole that's fallen down behind some bushes. We eat the chicken, pass the wine around till it's gone. Then we stretch out in the hot shade. I'm feeling pretty good. Bartlett is too. I can tell by the way he's smiling. I shut my eyes and snooze, and his voice buzzes as he tells the kid all about the Stumpy Sparrow Show. How one of the kids ate two many cookies and puked up chocolate chips in his lap. How he caught the pigeon and the cat backtage, sticking their tongues through each other's masks. He fired the cat and the pigeon quit and they ran off together and the next day Bartlett showed up drunk and dropped one of the kids off his lap and the station fired him. He makes it funny and the kid laughs and laughs. I take it he's feeling no pain. Then the kid tells Bartlett about the farm. He and his old man were putting up the storm windows and the kid dropped one and all the glass fell out and broke. His old man gave him a ration of shit, and the kid waited until the middle of the night and lifted fifty bucks out of his father's desk and started thumbing south so he could become a writer.

That night there are a couple of other people at Sal's. Old Elmore is one of them. After we go into the Evening Room he comes up and joins us three at the table. I see him checking out the kid and then he laughs a little and says, "Jim, your Mamma know you been hanging out with these birds?"

"Jim?" the kid says.

Elmore laughs. "Ah call everybody Jim." He reaches across the table and shakes the kid's hand. "Where you from, boy?"

"Maine."

"Whoooo!" Elmore says. "How you liking Florida?"

"It's warm," the kid says. He looks pale and his eyes are bloodshot. I'm guessing he's never drank Old Duke before and slept it off in the sun.

"He say it's warm," Elmore giggles.

Bartlett smiles at him.

"Warmer than Maine," the kid says.

"I expect it is," Elmore says. "Benjamin, what we smoking, honey?"

I hand him a cigarette and Elmore takes Bartlett's

and holds the red cone against his and lights it that way.
He blows smoke, looks at the kid. "They tell you all
about it, I suppose?"

"About what?"

"Don't be like that, honey," Elmore says. "About
the damn bird show. I know they told you. They tell
everybody else." He looks away, laughs inside his chest
so that it makes his head bob. With his dark face and
white whiskers he looks like Uncle Remus. We're quite
a gang: Uncle Remus, Stumpy Sparrow and Fat Benjamin. And this skinny little writer kid, who's looking
kind of green around the gills.

"Yeah, they told me," the kid says.

"Well, you believe these old birds?"

Bartlett and I look at each other.

"Yeah," the kid says.

"Shit!" Elmore says, "I guess I do too, then,
honey!"

When I wake Bartlett is coughing like he won't
ever stop. He's curled up on the cot, barking, stopping
only long enough to draw breath. I go over and put his
head in my lap, and start in thumping his back. But it
doesn't work. He keeps on barking until I yell at him to
stop. That doesn't help either. Ichabod hears the com-
motion after a while and opens the door.

"Call the ambulance!" I say.

He runs off and in ten minutes the door bangs open
and a couple EMTs come running in and take Bartlett
away from me. He's still coughing. He takes a breath
and coughs, takes a breath and coughs. They give him a
shot, and pretty quick he quiets down, and then after a

little while he seems to fall asleep. I get his sack and give it to the EMTs and they bring a stretcher in and take Bartlett away.

After breakfast I go outside.

It's already hot. My clothes are feeling damp and dingy. My heart's thumping in my chest. Old Elmore's talking to the kid at the curb. I go up and sit down with them with our feet in the street. Elmore twists his head around and says to me, "Don't you worry, he be all right."

I shake my head, look down at my fat fingers.

"Sure he will. That's a tough old bird. You wait and see. Hey Jim?" he says, leaning on the kid.

"Sure," the kid says. "He'll be fine."

"I don't think so," I say.

"What you want to talk like that for?" Elmore says. "That ain't gonna do nobody no good."

Cars blow by, washing us with hot air. Elmore stares at me, and when I don't say anything he nods. Then he grins at Barry. "What's on the agenda today?"

"I don't know," the kid says. "Is the truck supposed to come?"

"He say it is." Elmore tips his head back toward the building.

"Maybe I'll go pick."

"Make you some money."

"Uh-huh."

"Get you back to Massachusetts."

"Maine," the kid says.

Elmore squints at him, grinning.

We pick for a week because the kid wants to save

up enough for a bus back north. Meanwhile he wants to know all about Bartlett and his show, and I tell him everything I can remember, how Bartlett trailed the two of them across Florida, how he lost them here, in Tampa, and never left because he didn't have any idea which way to go. The kid writes it all down in his little notebook. Every night we stay at Sal's. Elmore's around some of the time, when he isn't laying up somewhere else. He's got some friends across town that he stays with on occasion.

Bartlett doesn't show, and we don't discuss where he might be. Then on the last night before the kid's bus, it's just me and the kid in the Evening Room when Ichabod comes in with a newspaper and lays it open on the table.

"I thought you might be interested," he says.

We look at it. There's a picture of Bartlett taken when he was maybe thirty, he's not looking too bad. In fact he looks pretty good, but you can tell it's Bartlett all right. We read the obituary. It's mostly about what a bad end this former TV personality came to.

The kid says, "So he was telling the truth."

"Evidently," the S.A. man says.

We look at the newspaper for a while longer. Then the S.A. man folds it back up and tucks it under his arm. He walks to the door and turns. "Gentlemen," he says, "you have a short time," and then he leaves and shuts the door. The kid goes to his cot, sits down and opens his notebook. He's writing like crazy. Then he lies down with his hands linked behind his head and now he looks impatient, like he can't wait to go to sleep so he can wake up and be on his way.

I sit at the table and wait for the lights to go out, and I miss Bartlett waiting there beside me, don't you think I don't. I look down at my big fat legs and try to come up with something of mine to tell this kid, for him to write down. Just so I can think about something else. I think way back in time. Back to when I was his age and before. I could tell him about my mother buying me books. They came in the mail every month in a little cardboard box. I wasn't so fat back then. I used to lie down in my bed and read Twice Told Tales and The Wind in the Willows and Huckleberry Finn and the other books she bought me and I could lie down then without worrying about it.

In the morning I walk to the Greyhound station with the kid. I'm huffing and puffing by the time we get there. When they call his bus over the PA he sticks out his hand and says, "I won't forget you guys."

I shake his hand. "It was nice to meet you."

The kid grins and walks through the doorway. At the bus he looks back at me. Then he hops up the steps. I wait until the bus pulls out and then head back to Sal's. It's hot, hot, hot walking through town. My clothes get all sticky and I shamble along pretty slow. I picture the kid in the air-conditioned bus, catching forty winks, heading back home. I wonder what he'll tell his old man.

I pass the bookstore on the corner of Elvira Street and look in the display window, and seeing all the books makes me wonder about the kid turning out to be a real writer, and then I wonder if he'll ever write all about his visit to Tampa and the Salvation Army. About Ichabod and Bartlett and Elmore and me. Picking oranges. Drinking cheap wine. I imagine us existing in a book that he wrote, and that book sitting in a display window somewhere. I imagine Bartlett coming back to life in his book.

I sit on a bench at the bus stop and look down the street at Sal's. It's a comforting idea and I want to sit here a bit and enjoy it. I stay put while a couple of buses stop, drive off. A lady with a shopping bag comes up to wait for the next bus and when she stands away instead of joining me on the bench, I understand and I'm not insulted. She doesn't know me from Adam. She just sees this big fat guy sitting there.

A bus pulls ups, its brakes hiss and the door swings open.

The lady gets on board and the bus pulls away into the traffic.

I sit there thinking some more on my new idea. I picture it so clear I can see the cover of the kid's book. There's rows of orange groves on the cover. There's sprinklers in the trees and rainbows in the spray. I picture a lady like the one with the shopping bag bringing our book home to her kid. Him lying in bed reading about me and Stumpy Sparrow and the Salvation Army and the orchards. My heart flutters with the idea of it all. This little kid's got a nice room and a nice bed with a thick pillow and a quilt. He lives up in Maine and it's snowing outside and he likes lying in bed reading. He's got a nice mother and a nice father. He's comfortable and he's not fat, and when he lies down on his back nothing comes up in his throat.

**Carnegie Mellon University Press
Series in Short Fiction**